A *Dire Wolves* MISSION

Savage Seduction

A Dire Wolves MISSION

ELLIS LEIGH

Kinship Press

Savage Seduction: A Dire Wolves Mission
Copyright © 2016 by Ellis Leigh

First Edition

ISBN
978-1-944336-06-6

Kinship Press
P.O. Box 221
Prospect Heights, IL 60070

Greed

*It is greed to do all the talking
but not to want to listen.*

— DEMOCRITUS

One

The dim, scattered lights inside the nightclub called to the shadows and left the crystal-trimmed rooms hovering closer to the dark side of the spectrum. The side where seduction ruled and things were not what they seemed. Each table, each nook and seat, sat blanketed in a haze of gray that hid truth and devoured logic. And that darkness lied. It lorded over the club in a deliberate way, disguising just enough sins for the human patrons to release their fears, to ignore what they knew, and to allow the shadows their falsehoods. They failed to see the filth and the lies through the darkness, the greed that wrapped around this place. That choked them all. But wolf shifters could see through the darkness, their animal sides refusing to give in to the siren's call of shadow and secret. And at least one did.

Dire Wolf Mammon sat in a dark corner nursing a beer, refusing to let the shadows seduce him the way they did the humans. Not immune per se, but stubborn. His inner wolf too damn strong to allow the human side to surrender to tricks of the mind. A good thing in a place like this.

Mammon's jeans and combat boots probably stood out in the crowd of sequins and sport coats, yet no one paid him any attention. Whether that was because he blended into the background as well as he did or the fact that nothing about him spoke of money and privilege, he wasn't sure. Maybe a little of both.

Probably a little of both.

"Can I get you another?"

Mammon tore his eyes away from the group of shifters across the bar and glanced up at the waitress. The blond hair and tight shirt seemed to be a uniform for the employees at this place, making her almost indistinguishable except by scent. He sniffed subtly, checking, making sure who he was dealing with. Ah, right…the good one. Kind, attentive, and hardworking, the woman before him had easily become his favorite employee. Some of the others…well, the drug scene in Fort Worth revolved around high-end pharmaceuticals, and the staff here had access few turned their backs on. But not this one; she smelled clean, untainted by the drugs and the liquor. If he'd been there for pleasure—not that he'd ever come to a place like this for pleasure—he might have flirted. Might have tried for a number or a quiet moment alone to enjoy the strategically placed shadows. But he was working in the club, as he had been every single night for far too long…as had his prey. Mammon was on a hunt, but not the kind that ended with a beautiful woman in his bed.

"Not tonight, but thanks."

"If you need anything—" she leaned in, giving him an exceptional view of her cleavage "—anything at all, just holler." She smiled before sashaying to the next table, leaving Mammon with an empty beer bottle, half a chub, and a serious need to accomplish something other than winning the award for most time spent in this den of inequities.

Fuck, he wanted those bastards across the club to *do something* already.

Mammon's phone vibrated in his pocket, a sure sign someone was trying to reach him and a distraction he didn't need. The caller was probably one of his brothers, his Dire Wolf packmates. Not Bez, though. No, the big, burly shifter with the light eyes and shorn head was too busy with his mate and their young charge to worry about what old Mammon was doing. Probably not Levi either. The kid who'd spent most of his life surrendering to a wanderlust few could understand had also found a mate, and with that, a permanent home in the mountains far north of the club where Mammon hunted. No, it was probably Phego, the brother who seemed the most concerned with Mammon's obsessions. Maybe Thaus, who'd spent a few months in the clubs with him, helping Mammon stalk his prey before he'd been sidelined by an injury from their last mission.

Both easily ignored.

The shifters across the bar suddenly cheered, holding up their glasses in a single-minded toast. What they were celebrating, Mammon didn't know. Deus, his tech-savvy brother with more computers in his pad than most people would own in their lifetimes, had worked his magic over his multiple keyboards but turned up nothing. Nothing too incriminating, at least. Sure, the group from New York were running some sort of pay-to-play protection circuit with the human businesses—old-school mob-type stuff Mammon had seen in action nearly a century before in New York and Philly—but that didn't explain their surge to power. Their money and status that seemed to have come from nowhere. The protection racket was small-time shit, which didn't fit their current lifestyle.

Those shifters from the Windy City were too rich for small time, too polished to be only in the business of taking money and cracking skulls. They were up to something bigger, and Mammon had spent almost two years trying to figure out what.

Trying…and failing.

His phone vibrated again just as the leader of the group, a man by the name of Finn O'Rourke, stood and grabbed his coat. If he was leaving, that meant the party would be over soon. He bankrolled their fun, led the charge for more drinks or fewer, and ruled over the members of his pack. Or at least, that's how it looked from the cheap seats where Mammon sat night after night.

Another vibration. Tearing his eyes away from the man he wanted to take down more than any other, Mammon ripped his phone from his pocket. He stared at the screen as his blood turned to ice.

Luc.

"Fuck," Mammon hissed before jumping to his feet, setting aside his fears with action. He tossed a bill on the table and rushed toward the front door. Luc—Dire Wolf leader, his pack Alpha, and one of the meanest motherfuckers Mammon had ever met—was trying to reach him. Luc never called. He hated technology, preferring to stay in the woods he loved so much and just show up when he knew he was needed. That psychic sense of his in relation to the six men of his pack was a finely tuned, accurate machine. If Luc was calling, something was definitely wrong.

Mammon's phone rang for the fourth time just as he reached his truck. He hopped inside and slammed the door—thankful he'd brought the old pickup instead of riding over on his motorcycle—before taking a deep breath. Probably nothing. Probably just checking in…for the first time in a millennium. He blanched as he swiped to answer. This could only be bad news.

"Luc."

"You were told to stand down."

Mammon bit back a growl. Challenging his Alpha wouldn't go over well. "Backing off was recommended to me, yes."

Luc apparently had no such qualms. His growl was as loud and clear through the phone as if he'd been sitting in the truck with Mammon.

"President Zenne feels it was more than a recommendation."

And there it was. The reason Luc bothered with the call. The Dire Wolves served at the pleasure of their president, one Blasius Zenne, known as Blaze to his friends. President Zenne ran the North American Lycan Brotherhood, keeping an eye on the various shifter packs across the continent and working with spoiled, arrogant regional leaders to enact rules and regulations that were supposed to better the lives of the average wolf shifter.

Mammon wasn't the biggest fan of rules and regulations. "President Zenne chose to close his eyes to the potential for chaos from this particular pack."

"Mammon—"

"They're out of control, Luc. Flaunting their wealth and power in every club in Fort Worth." Mammon sat back, quelling his anger as best he could. "The humans will notice. They'll want answers."

"And we'll deal with that when it comes." Luc's overly patient attitude only fanned the flames of Mammon's rage.

He gripped the steering wheel, trying not to punch through the damned thing. "If we sit back, it'll be too late. I know Blasius doesn't see this pack as an issue, but he doesn't understand the threat level. He's not here."

"You're not supposed to be there either."

The words stung a bit, the truth so plainly put something Mammon couldn't avoid. True, he wasn't supposed to be there. He was supposed to be farther north, checking in on packs in Oklahoma and Iowa for the NALB president. He was supposed to be working on official business, but instead…

"I can't just drop it, man." Mammon sighed, watching as Finn O'Rourke walked out of the club. The guy had three women with him, all tall and beautiful. All polished beyond belief. All very typical of what to expect from Finn. As the four stepped to the curb, a dark car pulled up, and a man jumped out to open the back door for the quartet. A perfectly orchestrated pickup resulting in zero wait time. A hell of a show, really. But Mammon knew nothing was that perfect.

Luc, on the other hand, didn't see what Mammon did.

"They're not a threat to us, Mammon." Luc's words weren't enough to steal Mammon's attention from the car as it drove off. Wasn't enough to set his soul right, either. Even if the man was sort of correct. They were, after all, the last remaining Dire Wolves. Their ancestry was one of legend, of myth and folklore. It carried an incredible weight. Dire Wolves…the oldest of the shifter breeds, the biggest and strongest wolves ever known, the most dangerous. Military trained, the seven were a badass group of shifters, all in closer contact with their wolves than other shifters. All skilled and dangerous in a hundred different ways. Few knew there were any Dires left in the world, for if that news spread widely, their shifter brethren could turn on them. It'd happened in the past—centuries before, halfway around the world. And an uprising would bring attention of the human sort, something no shifters wanted.

"Everyone is a threat to us."

Luc sighed, the static scratchy at Mammon's ear. "I've bought you two more weeks down there before Blaze comes for your ass. That's it—fourteen days, or I'll come down there to pull you out myself."

"Two weeks isn't enough."

If the growl Luc released was any indication, Mammon had pushed too far.

"Two weeks is more than anyone else would get, brother. You should be thanking Blaze, not flaunting your insubordination. Your special privileges won't last forever."

Truer words had never been spoken. Ever since Mammon had tracked down and destroyed a group of shifters threatening the NALB president from inside his organization—inside his very home—Mammon had been allowed a certain freedom. Given leeway on a few missions. But it seemed as if he'd run through that allotment of freedom.

"Fine," Mammon said, letting the growl he'd been holding back rumble through him. "Two weeks. I'll find something, a real sign that this pack needs monitoring, in two weeks."

"No games, Mammon. We've let you engage in your obsessive quest against the O'Rourke pack long enough. Get evidence, or get the fuck out. Don't make me have to hunt you down. And I'm sending in Thaus."

Motherfucker. "He's still healing from the incident in North Carolina."

Incident… Attack was more like it. Without Thaus, they never would have gotten Levi's mate back from the bastard who tried to take her. But the Dire had taken a bullet at close range to the shoulder, and his recovery hadn't gone as expected. Of course, it was too much of a stretch to believe Luc had somehow forgotten that fact.

"He can heal in Texas. Expect him, and know that if he issues an order, he's speaking for me," Luc said, growling through his words. "Two fucking weeks, Mammon."

The phone beeped as Luc disconnected, the tone final. As were Luc's words. Mammon kept his eyes trained on the doors, waiting for the rest of the O'Rourke pack to leave the bar. He even considered following them to see where they went after a night of spending and excess. But in the end, he threw his truck into gear and headed back to the apartment building where he'd been living since he started his investigation. He could have borrowed a piece of property from Blasius, could have rented a bigger place or something, instead. But the building filled with studio efficiencies was clean and safe, the units just enough for the shifter, the staff kind, and the owner the sort of person Mammon tended to surround himself with. Salt of the earth folks, ones without wealth and power.

The opposite of the fucking O'Rourke pack.

Two weeks…a lot could happen in two weeks.

Two

The sound of her bare feet hitting the shiny, wood floors rattled Charmeine more than she would ever admit. It was the sound of fear, of panic, of everything she fought against. A sound that brought back the worst of her memories, that haunted her most vivid nightmares. A sound easily disguised, but not yet. There simply wasn't time.

To keep from leaving without shoes, Charmeine yanked a pair of nude heels from a shelf in her walk-in closet and tucked them under her arm. Dresses, sweaters, and slacks came next, piles of clothes with designer labels that meant nothing to her. But they were required for her life, so she would make sure she brought them with her. When she couldn't carry any more, she rushed back into her bedroom and dropped the pile unceremoniously in front of her assistant.

"I only need the shoes right now." Charmeine grabbed the heels and slid them on her feet with a grimace. Not the most practical choice, but subtle. A pair that would match just about anything she chose to wear. A pair that would replace the soft pads of her feet with a clack that nearly echoed in the long hallways of her swanky Manhattan apartment.

But by God, did she hate them.

Ethan—her second cousin on her mother's side, her personal assistant, and the only family member she had left in the world—pawed through the pile of clothes, folding what he could before stuffing everything in a tan suitcase. Everything so very tan. "We need to be on the road in three minutes."

"I only need two." Charmeine rushed out of the room and down the hall, the harsh sound of her shoes a marked difference to the softer thuds from only a few moments before. She could already feel the change within her that the shoes inspired. She walked taller, straighter, put a little extra swing in her step. Her shoulders were back, her chin up, and her eyes focused straight ahead. She had a job to do. A part to play in the show that was her family's life and legacy. She would not fail.

But first, she needed to get out of the state. Alive.

Charmeine pushed open the door to the study and crossed the wool carpet lying under her father's heavy desk. He hadn't sat there for so long, not since the last time he'd been in their New York City home. Since the first time Charmeine had been forced to run for her life.

Without pausing to remember those better times, she pulled the family portrait off the wall. It was a good likeness of the three of them—her mother, tall and slender, blond and fair. Her father, bigger, though still fair and ever so handsome. And Charmeine herself in a color of pink she hadn't worn since the day the attacks had reached her family. The picture was one she'd spent many hours staring at over the years, wondering about the people who'd given her life, missing them immensely. It pained her knowing that painting would be in the trash within a few hours.

Picture frame out of the way, the ring in the drywall to open the secret panel became much more obvious, though essentially invisible to someone who didn't know it was there. Charmeine, though, had always known. Had been taught and trained on what to do on a night like this one from the time she was a little girl in pigtails. A wolf shifter too young to call her animal side forward and do anything to help when evil came knocking.

Focus. Run. Escape.

Panel open, the face of the safe stared back at her. Charmeine spun the dial for the correct number combination, then pressed her thumb to the scanner. When the first door unlocked with a soft clunk, she pulled it open and entered the second code into the keypad. A soft, blue light began to blink on the face of the fireplace, one hidden completely in the ornate carvings. Charmeine hunched over to look directly into it, letting the retinal scanner do its job. This time, the lock popped with a hiss, a release of the temperature-controlled air that kept the family's most important possessions safe.

"Time to go," Ethan called, the sound of his hurried footsteps disappearing down the hall. Charmeine didn't bother turning around. She had spent one minute, tops, opening the safe. She had one more before the danger truly escalated. Plenty of time for what she needed to do.

Stacks of money blocked the front of the compartment, a tease for anyone who happened to get this far. One she ignored. Charmeine pulled out every pack, dropping them to the floor without care. Bags of loose gems came next, then the gold and silver bars. All hitting the floor, probably damaging the wood and scaring her downstairs neighbors. Not that she cared any longer.

When the path was clear, Charmeine stepped up onto

the fireplace grate to reach into the back of the compartment. There, in a simple linen bag, sat the treasure she'd been after. The things she refused to leave behind. The things she would never forgive herself for losing.

Mission accomplished.

With barely a glance at the mess, Charmeine grabbed two stacks of bills just in case, pocketed the linen bag, and headed for the hallway.

Ethan met her in the formal foyer. "One minute."

"Told you I wouldn't need all three." Charmeine grabbed her sunglasses off the table and threw her purse over her arm. "Make sure Al knows to come deal with the money and gems in the safe. If the bastards leave anything."

"It could take weeks for him to get the trust set up so we can pull from that."

"We'll manage. There's no time to deal with it now."

The two headed down the elevator in tense silence. Three hired guards escorted them, not that Charmeine trusted them. In fact, there were only two people on earth Charmeine trusted. Ethan and Finn, one she was running with and the other she was running to. The two men whose families had been tasked with taking care of her after her parents' death.

No, not death. She refused to think of their end in such a generic manner.

After the slaughter of her parents.

The guards stayed close as they reached the lobby of the building, blocking Charmeine's view but leading her toward what she knew was the entrance. Forcing her to put her faith in them, no matter how hard she wanted to rebel at the thought. Once outside, the bulky men spread out a bit. Blocking the sidewalk, making sure the path from door to car was clear. Without a pause, Ethan and Charmeine strode across the concrete and slipped into the backseat of the dark town car idling at the curb.

Almost done.

The interior darkened considerably the second the door closed, the tinted windows blocking almost all light. One guard came around the driver's side and climbed into the back with them, another joining the driver in the front.

"Go." Ethan commanded the driver's attention with that single word. The car lurched into traffic, speeding down the avenue and spinning into a curve onto a side street.

"We did it," Ethan said, seeming relieved.

Charmeine wasn't so confident. "We'll celebrate once we're in the air."

She hadn't intended on staying in New York for much longer anyway, but the arrival of danger on their doorstep had rushed even her quick trip. Still, she needed to come, to close things up. To grab the last of her memories and say good-bye to her old life. It was time for new, time for different. Time for a change.

This wasn't their first time running, but hopefully, it would be their last.

As Ethan relaxed into his seat, Charmeine pulled her phone from her bag and tapped the messaging app, frowning as she typed a quick note.

The venue for the anniversary party must be changed.

The response from Finn was just as fast.

What did the hotel do and how can I help?

Not the hotel, the chefs. They refuse to cook in that kitchen.

Should I speak to the hotel manager?

Charmeine bit back a smile. Good old Finn, always trying to handle every detail.

No, I've taken care of everything.

When should I expect an update on venue?

Charmeine looked up, grabbing Ethan's attention. "How long is the flight?"

The smile he shot her was a slightly irritated one, and something she was quickly growing tired of seeing from him. "About three hours."

Charmeine went back to her phone, knowing Finn would be waiting for a response. *Give me thirty minutes. If I run into any issues, I'll contact Conner for assistance.*

I'll be waiting for your call.

The guard seated with them cleared his throat. "Discretion would make things easier, Miss Byrne."

Charmeine raised an eyebrow, wanting so badly to roll her eyes but knowing a Byrne could never be seen doing something so ridiculous. "Are you questioning my ability to work in secret?"

The guard, some hired human with a list of military titles longer than she could ever remember, looked a bit uncomfortable. Good.

"I wasn't implying—"

Charmeine's eyebrow nearly hit the ceiling. "Yes, you were."

"Someone sold you out," he replied, holding her gaze. An angry seriousness to his face. "Someone who knew where you'd be staying, what your plans were for the afternoon. Someone on the inside. I'm not calling you reckless, but the game has changed. Sending messages to anyone could be dangerous for your overall safety."

Charmeine could acknowledge when a man was correct, but in that moment, he wasn't. To prove herself—though why she felt the need, she'd never know—she tossed her phone to the man and sat back. "See for yourself."

His confused expression as he read the screen only made her want to smile. Smugly. Another thing she had to hold back. Her entire life had somehow become about restraint, a thought that didn't sit well with her.

Instead of smug, she pressed her lips into a flat line as

he handed her phone to a curious Ethan. "Finn and I never speak directly about the issues unless it's in person, and even then, our words are reserved. We have codes for everything."

"Parties and chefs?"

Charmeine shrugged, looking out the window as the boisterous city she'd rarely been able to enjoy flew by. Good-bye, New York. "Other shifters think I'm a rich, spoiled socialite with a tragic past. That language fits the assumption of me being a party princess."

Ethan glanced at the phone with a frown. "But what does it all mean?"

Charmeine hesitated. Ethan was family—a bit of a stretch, really, but the only family she had—but he didn't know everything about her. Not even close. Finn was the only person who knew more, and even *he* didn't know all. Secrets and lies, what her very few personal relationships were built on. But she couldn't let her guard down, not after decades of being hunted. Especially not after this day.

"It doesn't matter what each means." Charmeine took her phone back, slipping it into her purse once more. "All that matters is that Finn knows we're coming. He'll be waiting for us."

Ethan seemed irritated by her rebuff, but she couldn't worry about that. The guard was more than likely correct. Someone *had* sold her out, someone who knew her plans. If the police officer she'd secretly had in her pocket for the last eight years hadn't been so attentive, hadn't noticed the cars around the back of the building and the increased foot traffic heading into the basement of the high-rise, she could have been dead already. Her entire staff, dead. Her family legacy completely wiped out.

Something she could *not* allow to happen.

Charmeine crossed her legs and pulled a notebook out of her bag, forcing herself to focus on the work she needed to complete. The entire refugee chain had been alerted to the fact that someone knew her movements. Already, across the country, there were probably families on the run, all slowly converging on Fort Worth, Texas over the next few weeks. There were plans to be made, deals to put into place, and lives to save. Finn had been building a strong business front in the city for the past few years, a web of informants and hit men they would need to protect families targeted like hers had been. The ones who worried about every stranger, who built walls around every aspect of their lives in an effort to avoid the treachery of their enemy. Yes, Finn had spent two years setting up a place they could live and the protection they would need to do so, but even he hadn't planned on this sort of sudden migration from everyone in the chain.

Neither had Charmeine.

"We're going to need a building." She tapped her pen on the pad of paper before writing a task list that would be shared with her staff. "Ethan, pull up real estate listings. We'll need a big house, maybe a few guesthouses or outbuildings. A farm, perhaps? Somewhere close to open land would be nice for the children."

Ethan had his tablet out and ready, typing on the screen as she spoke. "It could take weeks to close. Should I look into immediate rentals for the interim?"

"Good idea. And we'll need supplies." Keeping her notebook close to her chest so the guard couldn't see what she was writing, Charmeine turned the page and started writing down a list of all the items they might need to house the desperate shifters they served. She wanted everything in place, the minutia of life acquired and stocked, before the first refugee child stepped foot on Texas soil.

She would not allow another family to be destroyed by the bastards who'd taken hers.

Three

It had always amused Mammon how humans considered certain days more social than others and therefore made it culturally appropriate to drink and celebrate on a weekday. Thursday night was a big one, if the crowd at the nightclub was any indication. Once again, he sat in the corner, nursing a beer and watching the young and wealthy shifters live it up across the dance floor. The only difference from the last time Mammon had sat in that exact spot being the leader of the pack across the way.

He didn't look as if he was having a good time.

Finn O'Rourke also sat tucked into a corner, though he had the comfort of a swanky, padded booth whereas Mammon's ass suffered in a wooden chair. One would think the most VIP person in the club would be having a great time, but that wasn't true for Finn. He sat slightly hunched over, scowling at the table. The man's highball glass should have shattered if looks could kill, and the members of his crew were all keeping a wide berth. Even the women he'd brought seemed to be avoiding him. Alone, Finn sulked in a corner, looking angry and completely absorbed by something other than what was happening in the club.

An interesting tidbit for sure. Mammon had two weeks left to prove the guy was as dirty as they come, and guys who looked as if their world was falling apart were usually easy targets.

Mammon pulled out his phone and shot off a quick text. Deus, with his knowledge of computers and information retrieval, could get his hands on more documents and classified information than Mammon would know what to do with. If anyone could figure out what was going on in the city that could distract a man like Finn, Deus would find it.

Four minutes and a fresh beer later, the response came in with a ping. Nothing. Nada. No word about bad deals in Fort Worth or any sort of situation that would result in a loss of income for the crime lord. Not exactly what Mammon wanted to hear, but he wouldn't give up digging. If only he could figure out a way to infiltrate the pack. To dig deeper into their protected little world and blow them up from the inside. That would be a major coup, sneaky and slightly over the lines Blasius had set for them, but deserved. The O'Rourke pack didn't play by the rules so neither would Mammon.

Hell, the O'Rourke pack didn't even seem to understand there were rules to be played by.

Normally, when a shifter pack moved into a town where an established wolf or pack had residence, they would approach with caution. Maybe introduce themselves. Feel out the locals and make sure they weren't crossing any claimed territory so as not to offend. Not the O'Rourkes. Finn moved in one day and started taking over the shakedown business the next. There was no local pack to speak of—not within a fifty-mile range, really—but Mammon had been there.

He was well known among the few shifters in the city. Finn should have given him the respect of an intro before taking over a job the human criminals in the area had handled for years. Not that Mammon gave a fuck about human criminals out of business—hell, he was glad for that. But Finn had handled his arrival in a way that screamed of disrespect and greed, two things that grated on Mammon's nerves. So he sat, and he watched the bastard, and he waited for a chance to prove his theories correct.

As Mammon took a drink of his beer, one of the raven-haired shewolves Finn had brought walked by. She tossed him a sultry look and a smile, both of which gave him an idea. He stood and followed her toward the back hallway, tracking her swinging hips like prey. If he could convince her to talk to him, maybe entice her to offer up a little info, he'd have an in. He wasn't proud of his plan, didn't like using a shewolf in that way, but desperation wasn't something he was used to dealing with. He could not fail.

But the woman wasn't alone in the hallway when he caught up to her. In fact, she was already in a serious conversation with another girl from the group. A conversation Mammon was happy to eavesdrop on if it meant getting what he needed. He settled against a wall a solid twenty feet away and pulled out his cell phone, looking to all the world like a man reading his emails or texts. Completely focused, just not by the device in his hand.

"Why tomorrow?" the woman he'd been following asked. "Can't they give us more notice?"

The other one, a blond nymph of a girl, shrugged. "Finn said she deserved a homecoming party, so he's throwing her one."

His target did not look pleased at that. "Wonderful. That's all we need—Charmeine Byrne coming to town and screwing up the pack order."

Nymph frowned. "She's not his Alpha female."

"But she sure as hell acts like it whenever she's around. He should just choose someone to help him lead, already. Our pack will never find balance under an Alpha male without a female by his side."

The clear jealousy and irritation from his target drew a throaty chuckle from the nymph. "He'd never pick you, so quit being catty."

The growl from the other woman nearly vibrated the walls, something even the humans could probably hear if any had been around. "He's my cousin. I wouldn't stoop that low."

Mammon bit back a laugh. Somehow, he doubted her protest would stand if Finn decided to choose an Alpha female. Hell, he was surprised the man didn't already have one. Leading a pack as big as the O'Rourkes almost required it. That was a definite weakness he hadn't known about.

The nymph sighed, seeming ready to head back to the party. "Look, quit complaining and come over tonight. I need to figure out what to wear. You know Charmeine will be dressed to the nines."

His original target sounded less angry when she answered, "Fine. What time's the party?"

"Seven. Charmeine and Ethan arrive tonight, though, so don't be surprised if you're summoned tomorrow morning for a greeting. I'm pretty sure all the O'Rourkes will be lined up at some point before the party begins."

The darker woman nodded, still scowling. "All this for a woman he isn't related to, mated to, or chasing after to get into bed. What is it with Charmeine Byrne that makes him obsess about her?"

Obsess? Mammon perked up, inching closer. Hungry for more information.

The nymph sounded almost sad when she answered.

"They grew up together. I wouldn't say he's obsessed… protective for sure, though."

"He has no business being protective—she may have been dropped off at their house when her parents died, but she's not an O'Rourke, and therefore, deserves nothing from us. But don't worry your pretty little head about me. I know my place, and I'll be ready for whatever Finn needs." The darker woman glanced in the mirror, running a finger along the edge of her bright red lips, catching Mammon's eye as she did. Shit…time to go.

A group of human females turned down the hallway, giving Mammon the perfect chance to slip back into the bar area without a lot of fuss. He dropped his unused phone back into his pocket and headed straight for the door. Mission accomplished. Tomorrow night…a party. The entire pack in one place and most likely distracted by the visitor and the intrapack wrangling for status. A perfect predicament for someone in his position. He wasn't fool enough to think he'd be able to sneak in, but he also wasn't about to let the opportunity pass him by.

Besides, since when did a Dire Wolf sneak?

If Mammon's two-year stakeout of the O'Rourke pack had taught him anything, it was that the group tended to be a bit scattered outside of the leadership. Finn ran the overall business and had some of the toughest, most intimidating shifters in the area leading the individual crews. Those guys were smart and savvy, and they were always ready with a fist or a claw if need be. But the rest of the O'Rourke pack, the hangers-on, were far more relaxed. A good thing, since apparently when Finn O'Rourke hosted a party, he put those relaxed people at the huge double doors that graced his ridiculous colonial estate. Seriously, did the man need so many white columns?

"You're here with who?"

Mammon gave the harried looking shewolf a gentle smile. "Colleen. I'm a guest of hers for the evening, but I ran a little late."

The girl sighed and flipped through the papers in her folder again. Mammon didn't know for sure if there *was* a Colleen in the pack, but with a surname like O'Rourke, the odds were pretty high.

"I don't see any of the Colleens with a guest."

Knew it. "Really? Maybe she forgot to add me." Mammon gave her a faux grimace, angling for a little sympathy. "Or she got mad about me being so late and figured this was a good way to punish me. She does seem to have a temper."

The shewolf snorted a laugh. "Don't they all?"

Mammon chuckled along, moving in for the kill. "A good woman deserves a man who is honest and respectful. This is all my fault for being late. Thank you for your time, but I think she's probably trying to teach me a lesson. I'll let you get back to work and try to call her later tonight instead. I'd hate to take up any more of your time."

He turned to leave, risking everything on that one statement. Then the girl sighed. *Jackpot.*

"No, no. No need for that. No sense kicking you out when you came all this way."

Mammon had to bite back his smug grin to keep up his charade. "Thank you so much. I'd hate to end up in more of the doghouse than I already am."

"Yes, well, depending on which Colleen… No. It doesn't depend. They're all a bit difficult." The girl stepped out of the way with a smile. "Welcome to the home of Finn O'Rourke."

"Thank you, miss." Mammon walked past her, through a doorway and into the house of the man he saw as his enemy.

No sneaking required.

The space was…not what he expected. With the way the man behaved in public, Mammon thought there would be opulence and sophistication in every corner. Instead, the large home seemed almost minimalist. Simple but modern, with clean, elegant lines as the overall design. Steel, leather, and wood dominated the space, not the Persian rugs and stuffy tufted furniture he'd assumed he'd find. Still ritzy, still way over what he'd buy for himself, just not as showy.

It wasn't often a person surprised Mammon. Finn O'Rourke had just accomplished that with something as simple as his decorating style.

Mammon followed the noise of conversation and laughing down a hall leading toward the back of the house. No one bothered him; no one questioned his presence. No one paid attention to the fact that he was not an O'Rourke.

For about three minutes.

The first shifter who seemed to realize Mammon wasn't supposed to be there was one of the dark-haired shewolves Finn brought with him to the club. She stared, her brow drawn down, her frown prominent. Mammon moved across the room, trying to stay casual in his pace, wanting to see a little bit more. There was no way he was going to get much intel tonight—that wasn't even the point, really. He had two weeks to finish up his investigation before Luc pulled his ass out of town. It was time to go balls to the wall. And by that, he meant a full-on infiltration of the O'Rourke network. Starting with Finn's personal residence.

The second person to seem to notice him was a big, burly shifter with dark sunglasses on his face, even in the house. Probably one of the crew leaders, a direct report to Finn. Not a good sign.

Mammon ducked behind a group of shifters arguing over something that sounded a lot like soccer and slipped into what appeared to be the room where all the action would occur. There was even a damned raised platform, like a stage or a dais. A little much, in his opinion, but exactly what he expected from a man like Finn O'Rourke.

The crew leader shifter followed Mammon, leading a group of similarly built men in dark suits. They spread out around the room then began to move closer, surrounding Mammon. Getting ready to snare a trap. Something he and his Dire brothers had done a million times themselves, though with a lot more finesse and disguise than Finn's crew. If the rest of the Dires were there—

But they weren't. Mammon was alone, a fact that amped up the tension already burning across his shoulders. With the beefheads caging him in, Mammon knew his time was almost up, but he had a point to make. One to the pack Alpha himself. A call to battle, if you would. So he stood his ground as the lights dimmed, and he waited for the show to start.

And start, it did.

To the cheers of his pack, Finn O'Rourke walked through a door at one side of the little stage. He stood tall and proud with a woman on his arm. Not a raven-haired beauty this time, though. This one had angel-light blond hair and a soft, fair complexion. The polar opposite of the dark-haired man at her side. Mammon didn't pay her much attention, though, too focused on Finn. Hoping the man took notice of the fox in the henhouse before the guards finally kicked his ass out.

But it wasn't Finn who noticed him first. It was the woman with him. The one the women at the bar had called Charmeine, he assumed. She caught his eye, and every atom of air evaporated, leaving him breathless in a sea of strangers who mattered not. There was no one in the room but her. Nothing that could call his attention away from her. There was only an angel of a woman standing next to a devil of a man.

Mate. Mine.

Mammon's wolf clawed at his mind to be let loose, to be allowed to shift and take control, but he fought the beast back. His mate, of all things. After centuries alone, after two of his Dire brothers had found mates in the last year, she stood before him. Watching him. Holding on to the arm of his enemy. A fact that caused his heart to drop into his shoes and his shoulders to sag under the weight of the truth.

The fates had a wickedly wrong sort of sense of humor.

"I'd like to welcome Charmeine Byrne to our Fort Worth home," Finn called, as loud and proud as he'd ever been. But Charmeine wasn't looking at him. She was staring at Mammon, a confused expression on her face. She knew, she felt it, but she had no idea who he was. And his time was up.

Two guards stepped between Mammon and the dais, between him and his mate, causing him to snarl in a decidedly dangerous way. Finn finally took notice of Mammon, and his smile fell into a look of utter rage.

"How the hell did you get in here?"

The room went silent. Mammon grinned, allowing the guard to grab his arm without resisting. It was time to go anyway. "You might want to get better security at the door."

Finn growled and moved as if to step down from the dais, as if coming to confront Mammon, but Charmeine placed her slender fingers lightly on his bicep. The man stopped, went completely still at the touch of Mammon's mate. A touch that made Mammon's wolf sit up and show his teeth. He didn't like his mate touching another male, especially a known criminal like Finn. A man she seemed to trust. A man about as opposite of Mammon as one could be.

Fuck, he was so screwed.

His mate finally stepped off the platform after a whispered conversation with Finn. The entire room remained quiet, their breaths held in anticipation as Charmeine approached with a cold sort of smile on her face. One that spoke of indifference and attitude. Of being above all those she passed. Still, Mammon couldn't look away. She was dressed like a woman of wealth—all silk, diamonds, and polish—with her hair perfectly in place and her makeup impeccable. No flaws to focus on, no scars to tell the stories of her life. No substance and certainly no soul that he could detect. Nothing he could see to make her worthy to be the mate of a Dire Wolf.

Except for the fact that she was.

"You got something you want to say, sweetheart?" Mammon gave her a smug sort of smirk, an arrogant tilt of his lips. He knew he shouldn't push her away, but he was at his wits' end. He wanted her in the basest way, his body responding to her nearness almost lewdly. But he hated her association with the O'Rourkes and was deeply disturbed that this woman could possibly be the one the fates had chosen for him. Dire Wolves were fighters, warriors, the strongest of the strong, and the most loyal of the breed. And Charmeine was…an associate of Finn O'Rourke.

A fact he couldn't look beyond.

When Charmeine finally reached him, finally stood close enough that he could smell the scent of freesia drifting around her spun-gold hair, Mammon stood silent and still. Anxious. Not knowing whether to grab her or run from her. Maybe both.

"I do have something to say, sir, though this won't take long." Charmeine gestured to the men holding him, a simple hand wave that had them releasing Mammon without question. "You follow my friend Finn, the family O'Rourke that I see as my own. You track them, keep tabs on them, and make them feel unwelcome in this town. Why?"

Mammon shrugged, still holding on to his smirk. Still

fighting back his need to kiss the ever-loving hell out of her. "Because I don't like criminals in my backyard."

Charmeine laughed, a tinkling sound that made Mammon's heart soar and his cock harden. Screwed, screwed, double screwed. He knew it, could sense the danger on the air around him. Especially when Charmeine fixed him with an icy stare that dampened what little heat had been sent southward.

"You come into this home under false pretenses and invade O'Rourke personal space, but Finn's the criminal? I think not."

Mammon tried not shiver from the way her voice slipped over his senses, but he failed. He failed hard, which only pissed him off even more. The woman would *not* get the better of him. "Look, Barbie. I'm not here to shit in your dream house. I'm just here to make sure the trash gets taken out at the end of the night. Preferably all the way back to New York where it belongs."

"Oh, dear," she said, raising her voice so the room could hear. Giving Mammon a glare that could have peeled paint from the walls. *Shit.* "It seems the fates have taken another jab at the Byrne family. They've chosen this" —her lips curled up in a sneer that did nothing to hide her beauty— "charming man as my mate."

The room positively vibrated with the energy of the other shifters. All eyes locked on Mammon, judging him. Sizing him up and finding him lacking, he was sure. But Charmeine didn't seem to notice. She leaned forward, giving Mammon a sight line down her form-fitting dress to the softest, most lickable cleavage he'd ever seen.

"Take a good look, sir," she whispered with a deadly tone to her voice. "This is the last chance you have. The fates may have tossed you at me like a raw steak toward a dog, but I'm no mindless animal. I get to choose, and I don't accept *you.*"

Her open hand slammed into the side of his face in a hard slap that would have probably sent a lesser man spinning. His mate had a strong arm. But Mammon jolted more at the venom in her voice than the slap, at the lethal warning under her words. The woman was *not* screwing around with him. Celtic Barbie had more to her than a pretty face. Much more.

And she looked as if she hated him.

"Get him out of this house." Charmeine turned and walked away without a second glance, leaving Mammon aching in more ways than one. "The O'Rourkes deserve a night to celebrate. I suggest we get to it."

Finn met her near the dais, shooting Mammon a curious look as he wrapped an arm around her shoulders. Whoever Charmeine was to him, he cared for her. Protected her. A fact that ignited a surge of jealous rage inside of him.

"Don't think this is over," Mammon said, making sure Finn heard the growl in his voice.

Finn simply shrugged. "It was over before you ever sat down to watch us in the clubs, shifter Mammon. Guards, please escort him out. Without harm."

As the men holding his arms forcibly removed him from the room, Mammon caught one last glimpse of his mate. She stood in the middle of a crowd of people, everyone clamoring and laughing. Calling her name and reaching for her hand as they congratulated her. She didn't smile back, didn't even seem to look most of them in the eye.

In fact, he'd never seen anyone look so alone in such a large group of people.

Charmeine stalked down the hallway, her stride long and her anger boiling over to the point that the metaphorical steam coming out of her ears clouded her vision. How dare the fates do this now? How dare they join her to someone when she was once again trying to rebuild her life? And to *that man*—the one Finn told her had been stalking his pack for close to two years. The nosy bastard…with the most gorgeous dark eyes she'd ever looked into.

No. She would *not* surrender to the magic of the fates. She wouldn't allow herself to fall into some mating haze or give in to the imperative to join with her chosen partner. She had work to do, shifters to help, and she was not about to let some egotistical asshole get in her way.

"Arrogant git." She growled and changed direction, needing to create distance between her and anyone else, wanting so badly to let her wolf out and run. But she couldn't, hadn't been able to simply let go in years. Not without Finn and his security detail by her side.

I don't like criminals in my backyard.

"*Stupid,* arrogant git." At least Finn's crimes were basically victimless. Plus, he targeted humans, not shifters. That distinction counted for something in her opinion. As did all the money he funneled to her to support her plans. God, without Finn…so many shifters would be dead by now, innocent men, women, and children who did nothing wrong but cross paths with psychopaths.

She'd be dead as well.

The clack of her heels on the stone floors was too much of a reminder of what had just happened in New York, of the fear and the running. Again. For years, Charmeine had lived on a never-ending loop of barely making it out alive whenever the Apex Hunters decided it was time to come after her again. And she was tired of it all.

"Charmeine."

Finn's voice behind her did nothing to slow her down. She knew he wanted to check on her, and she knew she'd need to talk about what happened eventually. But she wasn't ready. Not even close. So she kept stalking through the halls of his home, avoiding the other shifters there and doing her best to keep from exploding. But Finn followed her, of course.

Thank the fates she was with Finn when this silly mating happened, and that it was him tracking her down. He knew her, understood her in a way no one else did. He would let her come to grips in her own way and on her own timeline, even if he did refuse to let her be alone. His footsteps echoed just as much as hers in the empty halls, but he didn't move closer. A testament to the man's patience, really. He could have easily overtaken her—could have raced after her, caught her, and forced her to stop and face whatever he felt the need to say. Instead, he followed at a bit of a distance. Giving her the space to breathe. The opportunity to calm herself.

Not that it was working.

"How dare this happen now?" Charmeine asked as she reached a dead end in a dark and shadowed hallway. "I'm still not even able to walk outside alone, and we have all of these families converging on this town. A mating right now is the worst possible thing that could have happened."

"Not the worst." Finn leaned against the wall, looking patient and steadfast as always. "We have no control over matings. Fate doesn't ask our opinions."

Charmeine was not in the mood for that logic. "Well, fate can fuck right off."

Finn chuckled darkly. "Your father would be appalled at your language."

"No." She growled, rage making her heart race and her nails curve into claws as her wolf began to take control. "My father is dead, and not even you have the right to use his memory against me."

Finn's face fell, a look of pain streaking across his handsome features. "That wasn't my intention. I'm simply trying to contain—"

Charmeine's growl grew to a snarl. Finn stopped speaking, frozen in midsentence. Knowing he'd just screwed up. That word, that statement, was the absolute wrong thing to say.

"I will not be contained or controlled." Charmeine growled again and fought back her shift. Her joints ached as her inner wolf waged war against her human body, but she resisted. Suffered and wanted to cry, but resisted. "I am not some prize to be won, and I will not allow myself to be claimed by some…some…"

But the words wouldn't come. She wanted to call him a cretin, a Neanderthal, something disgusting and insulting. But her soul wouldn't allow it. He wasn't disgusting. He was handsome in the most base and rough way. Tall and muscled, thicker than most shifters she knew, with dark brown hair and a wickedly naughty smirk that made every inch of her take notice. But what had stunned her, what had nearly stolen her breath, was the depth in his eyes. The honesty she could almost feel there. He had snagged her attention with that one look, made her practically shake with a need that pulsed and burned…and didn't that just piss her off even more?

Charmeine huffed and took off again, heading for the suite of rooms Finn had offered her when she'd arrived. He followed, of course, because he always followed. He never let her hide from the situations around her. A most irritating trait, but one that had kept her alive. So far.

She stormed into her room but continued to pace, growling and snarling as her thoughts went from what her new mate was—handsome, daring, intriguing—to what he had to be—enemy, dangerous, deadly. Finn leaned against the doorway, watching her. Waiting her out. They'd been too close as children, too tied up in the hell their lives had become to make many friends. They were as close as siblings and just as stubborn. She knew he'd wait for days if necessary; he was patient like that. And he knew she needed time to rein in her anger. To get the fire burning in her soul under control.

But all fires eventually burned out, including ones set by the fates. Charmeine crumpled onto the edge of the bed and stared at the ground. Unable to find a path to take in her head.

"What do I do?" Her voice was too soft, too broken and weak. That wasn't what she wanted to sound like. She'd battled madmen, saved shifters from certain death, and run a secret rescue organization for victims of the Apex Hunters for years. She was *not* weak.

And yet, this situation sapped her inner strength. Meeting her fated partner hadn't been something she could have prepared for. Nothing she'd expected. She'd found her mate…in an enemy.

Finn pushed off the wall, walking toward her casually. Slowly. That O'Rourke charm in full effect. "Maybe it's not as bad as it seems."

"Your enemy is my enemy, and you told me that man has been watching you for years. That's an enemy, Finn. We both know it." Charmeine's returning glare should have made him take a step back, not grin at her as if she were a stubborn child. She growled and twisted to the side, lying on the bed in an almost fetal position. Finally settling into something close to a non-raging state. "Why now? Why him? How dare the fates screw this up so badly?"

"I have no enemies, save one." Finn knelt before her, reaching for her hand. "He is not a danger to us. Maybe you could give this mating a chance."

"Are you trying to get rid of me already?"

"Never. But what kind of life will you have with me? Gaming humans to support our adopted family? Constantly looking over our shoulders for Apex Hunters?" He sighed, staring at her hand as he ran his fingers over the back of it. "This man—he's not like them. He could have acted on numerous occasions, but he didn't. He watched, but he didn't attack. I can't blame him for being concerned about my pack considering how I moved in here, really."

"Finn—"

"He was here first. I didn't seek him out, nor did I inform him that I was bringing a pack with me. That's my fault. He's watched my group and me ever since, has avoided me whenever I've attempted to engage him in conversation, but he's never acted against us. He's never made a move to hurt this family, not even by slipping into our home uninvited. I don't think he's as dangerous as he is…pissed and insulted." Finn sighed and brought her hand to his lips for a simple, single kiss. "As much as you think he's against us, and as much as you don't trust him, you can't deny the fates have offered you a gift, Charmeine."

Charmeine pulled her hand away, a spark of temper growing once more inside of her. "They've offered me a life sentence of servitude."

Finn chuckled and kissed her forehead before hopping to his feet. "My mother was not in servitude to my father, and nor was yours. Our parents loved one another deeply. Perhaps that sort of future is what the fates are offering you today." He paused at the door, looking back at her with eyes so dark and pained, they made her catch her breath. "We deserve a break, Charmeine. We have scrambled for simple survival for too long. Fated mates are so very rare, it seems. We haven't had a proper mating in the family for coming on twenty years now. I had begun to think I'd destroyed the O'Rourkes with all of this questionable activity, but apparently, the veil of bad luck has lifted. At least for you."

"I don't believe in luck," she whispered, her heart practically in her throat.

But Finn always could see through her lies. "Think about it then. See if there isn't some small part of you willing to at least give the man the fates chose to be yours a chance."

Charmeine waited for him to close the door before she rolled over to bury her face in the mattress…and scream. A chance? No. Chances meant risk. She couldn't hinge her life on the possibility of something as fickle as luck or chance or…something else not of her own making. She couldn't leave the families who relied on her to go chasing dreams she'd never really cared about anyway.

Okay, that was a lie. She remembered how happy her parents had been. How much they adored one another. Their mating had been a gift and a blessing, and they'd lived each day basking in the love they shared. She wanted that.

Wanted to know what that sort of connection to another person felt like.

But not like this.

Not this guy.

No matter what Finn said, Mammon was a threat. And she refused to accept a mating to a man who could finally destroy her world.

The fates were assholes bent on making people miserable.

Mammon peeled out toward his place as if he was being chased. His turns were too sharp, his grip on the accelerator too tight, making the bike rev to a level that crept a little too close to the red line. But he was pissed and needing a release, and pushing his sport bike to the absolute limit was better than any of the other things he could do to blow off steam.

Every thought in his head centered on one thing, every fear pushing him to ride harder, go faster, hinged on the same fucking thing. Charmeine…his mate. His fated match, the only one he'd ever have. Just the thought of her name had him driving harder in his rush to escape her clutches. Not that she was clutching. Not really.

Okay, not at all. The woman was about as far from clutching at him as could be. Kicking him out was more like it.

"Un-fucking-believable." Mammon dropped low over

the tank as he hit the highway, maxing out his engine on the entrance ramp. He was running—something Dire Wolves never did—and didn't that thought just chap his ass? But how was he supposed to deal with the pile of shit the fates had thrown in his lap? She was his enemy's…friend? Lover? A disgusting thought on so many levels but one that would have to be addressed at some point. Perhaps Charmeine and Finn were business partners. Easier to digest, but still an issue. He couldn't trust someone who stood at Finn O'Rourke's side the way Charmeine had. No way. She was an enemy by association at the very least.

And yet, the draw to her, the pull to turn around and find her, was almost too strong to ignore. Mammon clenched the grips tighter and stormed down the highway, hating that he had to consciously think about where he was going so he didn't instinctually turn the bike around and head to the O'Rourke's place. Hating that one chance meeting had taken so much control from him.

He despised being mated.

When Mammon finally leaned into the curve that would bring him to the parking lot at the place he considered home, Phego's truck sitting right next to his just pissed him off even more. Why the bastard needed to be there, Mammon had no idea. But he knew he wouldn't like it.

He trudged up the stairs and to the door marking his tiny claimed space in the world, dreading having to deal with his Dire brother. This entire day had gone to hell, and he couldn't even get a night alone to break shit and get drunk. Wonderful.

Mammon stormed inside his little rented studio apartment and slammed the door behind him. Phego stayed sprawled on the couch, his feet resting on the end table Mammon usually used as a dinner table. Feet up, propped against pillows, and watching the small television on the dresser, the fucker looked to be the picture of cool and relaxed. Mammon knew better.

"What do you want?"

Phego didn't even twitch. "Deus called me in a panic."

"Deus doesn't panic."

Phego lifted a shoulder in a lazy shrug. "Fine. He called me in about as much of a panic as I'd ever heard from him. Seemed like you'd gone into enemy territory alone, and he wanted someone to run backup in case you needed help getting out."

Fucking computer expert and his need to microchip the phones of each Dire *just in case*. Tonight had not been a just-in-case moment. "I didn't need help."

"I know. I was there when you left." Phego wasn't one to mince words, but even for him that statement dropped with a weight that just about shattered what little control Mammon had left.

Slow and predator-like, unable to stop himself from stalking the man he saw as his brother, Mammon crept across the room. "You were there?"

"Your mate is very pretty."

And there it was, Mammon's truth laid bare in five little words. There would be no hiding from this, no avoiding it. The Dire Wolf pack would all know simply because that's how they were. No lies, no running away when things got rough, no avoiding the reality of any predicament. No going into dangerous situations alone. There was no way Mammon could live up to those expectations when it came to Charmeine. Not at all.

"Shit." Mammon picked up an almost-empty water bottle and threw it across the room, denting the wall. He'd have to fix that at some point, but seeing drywall crumble to the floor was oddly satisfying. Totally worth it.

Phego, on the other hand, just relaxed into the couch

cushions, looking completely calm and collected. "Deus is pulling information on her now. Phone numbers, addresses, anything he can find. You'll have it in a few hours. You should call Bez."

"No."

Bez was too far into his own world, having been with Sariel for well over a year. The man would tell Mammon to go back, grab his mate, and drag her home like some sort of caveman. Not happening.

Mammon stomped to the kitchenette in the corner. Though calling it a kitchenette was giving the space grand goals to live up to. It was more of three tiny cabinets with an even smaller sink, a mini refrigerator, a microwave, and a coffeemaker. And his supply of liquor.

"Call Levi."

Mammon paused, Jack Daniel's in hand. That idea had merit. Levi had just found his mate a few weeks ago, had stumbled on her in the middle of a mission just like Bez when he found Sariel. Mammon still had a slight divot in his arm from where he'd been shot as Levi, Phego, Thaus, and he worked together to save Amy from some crazed shifter and his human friends. It'd been hardly any time at all, really, which meant mating was just about as new to the kid as it was to Mammon. Okay, not really, but still. Close enough.

Mammon's phone was in his hand before he realized he'd even taken it out of his pocket.

The line rang three times, an excessive amount in his opinion, but then the voice he wanted to hear came through the speaker.

"What's doing?"

Mammon had never been more relieved to hear those two words from the kid. As he began to pace the length of the room, the entry door snicked closed. Phego had left without a word, giving Mammon the privacy he needed for a call like this. A fact Mammon appreciated.

"I need to talk to you, kid."

"Okay." Levi's voice turned wary, cautious. He knew something was up.

"I…" Mammon paused, took a deep breath, closed his eyes, and said the words he needed to. "I met my mate tonight."

"That's awesome news!" Levi's excitement nearly made Mammon drop the phone, but he didn't. He held on, wishing he had led with a different line.

"Stop, man. It's…not so awesome."

"Why not?"

Another breath. Another second to make sure his words came out in the right order. Without expletives. "She's a personal *guest* of Finn O'Rourke."

"Oh…so she's like…I mean, maybe she's not his…well, shit."

"Yeah. That was about my reaction." Mammon sank to the floor with his back to the end of the bed. "I don't know what she is to him, but she's close enough to be staying in his house and get a personal introduction party hosted there."

"Could be related," Levi grunted before Mammon could respond. "That'll make for some awkward holiday dinners."

Sighing, Mammon dropped his head on the mattress to stare at the ceiling. Blank white space stared back…a nothingness he felt all the way to his toes. "I can't go through with it."

"What are you talking about?"

"The mating. There's no way I can trust someone who has a relationship with my enemy."

Levi's sigh caused a rush of static over the line but not enough to hide the frustration in his voice. "He's not your enemy."

"Bullshit," Mammon responded, the words hard and direct.

Levi sighed again, the asshole. "You've had a hard-on for that pack for two years now. Ever stopped to wonder why?"

The eyeroll Mammon performed could have won an award for epicness. "Uh, because they're criminals invading my home?"

"If that were the only reason, you'd have requested an investigation and let the Feral Breed or the Cleaners handle it. But you didn't. You staked them out yourself between missions, even though you never acted on a single thing. Why is that?"

The kid had a true talent for pissing Mammon off. "I don't know, genius. Why don't you tell me?"

"Tell you? Shit, man—I don't know. I'm just making conversation."

Mammon's snort of laughter couldn't have been stopped if he'd tried, not that he did. "Fucker."

"Yeah, I am." Levi's voice dropped, becoming more serious. "I'm a fucker who claims his mate as often as he can because he loves her and can't stand to be away from her for long. How're you feeling about *your* mate right now?"

Mammon sighed, the sound turning to a frustrated growl. How was he feeling? Like he wanted to run back to O'Rourke's house and fall to his knees before her. Like he wanted to grab her by the arm and yank her away from that place. Like he wanted to give up everything to have her or maybe give up everything to run from her. In other words, he was fucked.

"That's what I figured," Levi said. "Look. The fates don't mess around with this stuff. My need to be with Amy was, and still is, ridiculous. It eats at me. I could barely resist her before we exchanged mating bites, so I'm not sure how you can possibly think you're not going to fall for it."

"I can resist."

"Liar. But go ahead and try. You'll be miserable. But you know what's worse? You'll make her miserable."

Mammon's stomach plummeted, and his heart actually ached. As much as he hated the O'Rourkes and everything they did, he didn't want his mate miserable. Not for a single second.

"Shit." Mammon ran a hand over his face, trying to clear away the thoughts of Charmeine so he could focus on finding a solution. Instead, all he could see, all he could think about, was her face as he was being pulled away. The sadness, the wall. The loneliness. "Are you happy, Levi?"

"Ecstatic." Levi's answer was too bright, too quick. Mammon had trouble believing him.

"I mean there…in Hope Ridge. Locked down in some small town after being on your own and free for so long. It's different than the life you lived before her."

"Different, but not in a bad way. Amy's teaching me about roots and making a place for yourself. Her pack is a lot of fun, and her brothers—all fucking twelve of them—have taken to trying to beat me at wrestling. It's sort of awesome being able to kick their asses without getting into trouble. But even if it wasn't fifteen levels of A-OK? Even if her family hated me and this town felt like a prison? It wouldn't matter."

Mammon knew what the answer would be, but he had to ask the question anyway. "Why not?"

"Because I'd have Amy by my side. She makes everything worth it." And there it was, the truth Mammon had no idea what to do with.

"Point made, kid."

"Good. Now get off the phone and figure out a plan to get your mate. I'm down for an extraction or retrieval if need be. Just call."

That was a Dire Wolf for you—newly mated but ready to

battle beside his brothers. Mammon couldn't have asked for a better team. Which was why he felt comfortable admitting his fear. "I'm pretty sure she hates me. She fucking slapped me right in the face tonight."

"A real slap?"

"My jaw still stings a bit."

Levi chuckled. "Hate sex can be hot, old man. Just go for it."

Mammon laughed right along with him, feeling a million times more centered than he had when he'd initiated the phone call. Still negative, but on solid ground once more. "Go be all happy and shit, kid. I've got stuff to do."

He swiped to disconnect the call and tossed the phone on the bed. Pictures of his mate, of *Charmeine*, cycled through his mind. Her silky hair, her pale skin, the fierceness in her eyes. The brave way she didn't let Mammon pull any shit on her. She was like some sort of warrior, defending her land and home. And fuck him if that wasn't hot.

Without thought to the action, his hand slid down past his waistband. Pressing into his cock over his jeans. Every picture, every thought, focused on his mate. His *mate*. The one woman the fates chose who would complete his life. And even though he thought that was some bullshit still, he couldn't resist the idea of her and him…*mating*. He wanted to see if her skin was that pale all over, if those curves she'd hidden beneath her dress felt as good as they looked. Wanted to know what she tasted like and how her body would react when he made her come.

Pants undone, hand sliding underneath to grip his hard cock, he gave in to the temptation. To play, to imagine, to fantasize. Just once. Just this one time he'd jack off to thoughts of his mate. Then he'd stop so he could focus on figuring out a way out of this mess. Because he would get out of it—he had to. No matter how happy Levi seemed, this was a different situation. A doomed one.

Fingers sliding, hand gripping, he tugged and pulled and thrust until he came all over his own hand. Until thoughts of ice-blond hair and big, blue eyes brought him to his figurative knees.

When he was through, spent and panting as he sat on the rough carpet, he dropped his head back again and stared at that white ceiling. At the nothingness it represented.

What the hell was he going to do to break this mating?

Charmeine stared out the window, refusing to touch her oatmeal. Finn sat across from her as he had every morning since the party, attacking her choices in that niggling way of his. The man was a bulldog, completely unable to let go of something once he zeroed in on it. He pushed and prodded while she stood fast to her convictions and plans. Two people at opposite ends of the fight. Neither making any headway at convincing the other.

The breakfast table had become a battleground.

"Think about it," Finn cajoled, trying so hard to sound gentle. Persuasive. But Charmeine saw through his façade.

"No."

Her answer hadn't wavered in days, not since the night her mate had barged into Finn's house to make some sort of point. She'd stopped expanding on her refusal, sticking with a one-word answer that should have been enough to make Finn stop harassing her.

Should have…but wasn't.

"Damn it, Charmeine." Finn threw his napkin on the table, glaring her way.

That just wouldn't do. "I can't trust him, Finn."

"He's your mate."

"Did that save your aunt Fiona?"

Her words were clipped, harsher than they should have been, but she needed to make her point. She remembered Finn's aunt well. The woman had mated to a man their pack had seen as an enemy, too. That man had come into the O'Rourke family—been welcomed, even—and had made a place for himself for a number of years. But then the Apex Hunters got to him, and he sold out the family just as a stranger would have. Fiona O'Rourke was killed in the fight, Finn's parents both injured. And Charmeine had lost her belief that the fates were anything other than liars.

No, Charmeine didn't see mating as the trust-builder Finn did.

But the man was nothing if not stubborn. "You can't compare all men to that traitor."

Charmeine cocked her head, thinking over his words. And dismissing them. She could, she absolutely could. "The Apex Hunters have been slaughtering us for centuries. Bringing in outside help didn't stop them, trying to hide didn't stop them, being mated didn't stop them…nothing stops them, Finn. I refuse to put my friends—what little family you have left—up for target practice simply because the fates think this…*man*…is a good fit for me."

Finn sat back, eyeing her coolly. "And if he's not the enemy?"

Charmeine swallowed back the hope that grew at his words and seemed to warm her heart. The emotion she couldn't give in to for a single moment. "He's been watching you for two years, if not longer. If he's not in with the Apex Hunters now, he will be soon."

"We've gone two decades without a single fated union, and you want to ignore yours. Why must you be so pessimistic?"

Charmeine huffed a laugh. "Realistic is more like it. The bastards won't pass up the sort of knowledge one gets from stalking a pack like yours."

Finn shrugged, a move that looked far too forced to be believable. "He never acted on anything."

"Until he walked into your home three nights ago." Charmeine shook her head, nearly growling in her anger. Fighting hard for her last sliver of control. "They will find him, and then he'll be a weapon against all of us."

Finn sat quietly for a few moments, contemplating something only he could see. "The Hunters have done the whole mate-as-traitor thing. They won't repeat themselves."

"That's a chance I'm not willing to take." Charmeine tossed her napkin over her bowl, too angry to even think of eating. Those were hard words said in a tone she'd never used with Finn before. Sounds that showed her anger but focused on her fear. She would need to rein herself in if she was going to keep the rest of the family calm. Brave faces led confident troops.

Finn grew quiet again, staring out the window as Charmeine ignored her oatmeal. He was right—the Hunters never pulled the same tricks twice. They liked to give the O'Rourkes a few years of peace before showing up unannounced in some new and deceptive way. They seemed to enjoy the spy-game aspect of their hunt more than anything. Except the killing. She remembered well the night her parents died. What those murderous bastards did to them. The Hunters definitely enjoyed the killing.

"Is it worth it?"

Finn's question pulled Charmeine from her brutal memories. "Is what worth it?"

"This. The life we're both stuck living. My running this business."

"Of course, it is." Her words were automatic, but her brain still snagged on the thought. Worth it? Worth what? Because she didn't remember much from a time before the Hunters had blown her life apart.

Finn rolled his eyes, probably seeing right through her as he always did. "It's very public, what I do. I thought perhaps that would keep the Hunters from trying anything, but then…"

He trailed off, but Charmeine knew where his thoughts had gone. As well as he knew her, she knew him the same. There was no hiding from each other.

"But then we got word that they'd infiltrated my New York world, and I had to run again."

"Exactly." Finn frowned. "I wanted so much more for you than this. I wanted better for both of us."

Charmeine was up and moving toward Finn before he even finished his sentence, sliding her arms around him from behind the second she drew near. "Your business dealings keep the last of your family safe. The money keeps them hidden so they won't be murdered in their sleep like the ones before them. Your team has built a fortress of protection around this city with informants in every corner. This is the safest any of us have been in decades."

Finn gripped her forearm, holding on to her like a lifeline. "But is it enough? When will it ever be enough?"

Charmeine shifted forward, dropping to her knees at his side so she could meet his tortured gaze. "For the past six years, we haven't lost a single soul. In fact, we've grown. There are children running around, cousins playing together. New generations brought into the world all because you were brave enough to chase your idea of setting everyone up in one area that you protected. A city you ran, where we could all live normal lives. That's what you're working for."

"And yet, we're still alone. Well, I am." He sighed, grasping her wrist to pull her into his lap. "I want this fated union to work for you. You're practically my sister, and to see you happy and protected would bring me nothing but joy. But I can understand your hesitancy, and I will try my best not to push again."

"Good." She kissed the top of his head and cuddled closer, the two sitting in one chair as they had a million times before. Comforting each other in times of stress and hardship.

Eventually, though, Finn pulled away with a sigh, helping Charmeine back to her feet before rising to his own. "I'm sorry to be so abrupt, but I have some business to attend to. You'll be all right by yourself?"

Charmeine pasted her customary smile on her face, a force of habit too hard to break. "Of course. You go work. I'll be fine."

Finn shook his head—seeing through her as usual— but didn't call her on it. Instead, he kissed her cheek before heading for the door. "You should go for a run. Your wolf needs to be let out."

"Soon, perhaps." She ignored the whine from her inner beast. That lonely, sad sound would do them no good. Finn's security detail was stretched thin enough. She didn't need to add to their burden for something as selfish as a run.

But there were moments, like right then, when she really wanted to.

The second the smack of his dress shoes on the stone grew too far away to hear clearly, Charmeine sank into his chair, letting the smile slide from her face. Alone again. The aching sense of being the last ship in the storm had followed her from New York, whispering in her ear about her failures and fears. New York had been busy, active, a city you could almost hide in. But here…

Here there was so much to do, but far too much to worry about getting in the way.

She needed to work. First project being securing accommodations for Finn's family, the ones converging on the area. Already—with barely a handful of refugees having arrived—Finn's house was far over capacity. She needed to find a rental property to house them all quickly. And then there was *him*. The man Finn had called Mammon…her mate. The bond she hadn't been expecting. What a cruel joke, to offer up something as wonderful as a mating to someone as cold and closed off as she. What were the fates thinking? She had no time for such things—and definitely not the ignorance to give in to her attraction and risk the lives of those who relied on her. No. There would be no mating, no matter how much that thought made her wolf want to howl mournfully at the moon.

"Charmeine?" Ethan leaned in the doorway, looking a bit wary. She'd been putting him off for the past three days, too focused on the drama around Mammon to concentrate on work. But that ended. Now.

Charmeine pasted her smile back on. "Yes?"

"I have three rental properties to visit this morning, and I wasn't sure…"

Charmeine brushed aside thoughts of matings and families and the harsh losses she'd seen from both to concentrate on the future. The growth. The blessings they had worked so hard to earn. "Of course. Let me clean up, and we can go."

Ethan seemed surprised, though pleasantly so. "Very good. I'll wait for you in the foyer."

Seven

They're not coming."

Mammon shot a glare at Phego. Why he'd chosen the Dire as his partner on that night's stakeout, he was beginning to wonder. "You have a gift for the obvious."

But still, his brother's words ate at Mammon. He wanted the O'Rourkes to come, needed to see his mate once more. He'd been jonesing for a glimpse of her for days, which was why he'd talked Phego into coming to the club with him to watch the criminal group. He hadn't mentioned mates, but he had a feeling Phego knew exactly why he'd wanted to sit in this dark, loud pit that night. It wasn't for justice or to keep an eye on the bad guys—no, it was for one shewolf who had Mammon's world flipped upside down. Charmeine…she who had somehow sunk her claws into his flesh and wouldn't release him even as she kicked him away. He wanted her, needed her like a junkie needed a fix. And he fucking hated that.

But obviously, he wasn't going to get his hit of the sight

of her that night. The entire O'Rourke pack was noticeably absent from their favorite scene. Something Mammon would have been thrilled for a month ago, but now…well, it sucked. And he fucking hated that even more.

Phego almost smiled, though, a true accomplishment for the taciturn shifter. "You planning on popping over to their house again?"

A low, and yet truthful, blow. Mammon growled, irritated by the sudden howling of his wolf as the idea of tracking his mate floated through his thoughts. Traitorous little shit.

"No. Not at all."

"Then I'm out." Phego stood, grabbing his phone from his pocket as he stepped around the table. "Tomorrow."

"Sure," Mammon said, peeling the label off his half-filled beer. "I'm just going to finish this and take a piss before I go."

"You do you." And with that, Mammon's brother left him at the table. Alone. Staring at nothing.

"You are a sorry son of a bitch," he murmured, but beer bottles didn't make good listeners. Mammon dropped the bottle on the table and headed toward the back of the bar where the restrooms were. It was time to call tonight as a failure. He could regroup with Phego in the morning and figure out a better plan to…track the O'Rourkes. Not stalk his mate. His focus was on the O'Rourkes. And one Byrne.

Shit.

Three minutes of a stern talking-to in the men's room mirror and a set of washed hands later, Mammon walked outside into the crisp night air. He'd only had the one beer, and in fact hadn't finished it, so he had no qualms about driving. At least not until he turned the corner.

A dark town car idled in front of his motorcycle. The same kind of car he'd seen Finn O'Rourke whisked away in a few days back. The night before Mammon chose to go to the guy's house…the night before Charmeine.

Double shit.

Mammon knew what was coming, who would be waiting for him, before that back door even opened. Still, as Finn O'Rourke stepped out onto the concrete, his heart thumped a little faster and hope caused his mouth to go dry. He couldn't help but attempt to look into the car, to see if someone else was with the wily fucker. A particular shewolf, for example. One he shouldn't crave as badly as he did. Fucking mating instincts.

"I think we should talk," Finn said as the Dire approached. Mammon kept his face neutral, his glare hard. No sense giving this guy a single inch.

"And why's that?"

The fucker had the nerve to smile. "Are we going to play coy here? I thought we could handle this as men."

"Well now, that depends."

"On what?"

Mammon went toe-to-toe with the man, looking down on him, pulling his wolf forward so his eyes would swirl silver as only the Dire Wolves could do. "Only if you've got big enough balls to deal with me directly."

Finn didn't flinch, didn't lose his cool. He stared back into Dire eyes, into the face of a beast long thought to be extinct, and stayed his course. Something that secretly impressed Mammon. But the guy did open his mouth.

"You're mated to my best friend."

And just like that, all the bravado Mammon had fronted with faded away. He took a step back. Then another. Then he shook his head. "Not sure what that's got to do with you."

Finn's smile turned to a scowl, the wolf side of the shifter making himself known in a rumbly growl. "She's practically my sister, that's what. She's also hardheaded and stubborn, much like yourself, I'm guessing."

Mammon nearly sighed in relief. If Charmeine was like a sister to the man, that meant they probably weren't in a physical relationship. Which was good. One issue he could stop obsessing over. Ninety-eight to go.

Not wanting to show his hand, Mammon chuckled and leaned against the side of the car. "Hardheaded and stubborn? You've got me there."

"Then join me in my car so we can have a conversation. I'll have my driver circle the area while we talk, and then bring you back to your bike."

But even knowing they'd be talking about the woman he'd found himself mated to didn't wipe away his distrust of anything and anyone having to do with the name O'Rourke…especially the patriarch of the family. "And why the fuck should I believe you?"

"I'm a thief but not a liar." Finn shrugged and held up his hand, two fingers raised and pressed together. "Scout's honor."

Mammon had to bite back a laugh. The shifter had moxie, that was for sure. "Pretty sure you were never a Boy Scout."

"True, but I do have honor, and I would never do anything to upset those I care about. Losing her mate would upset Charmeine, so you have my word that I'll make sure you return to your bike in the same shape as you leave it." His eyes were true, strong, showing his bravery in the face of a bigger wolf. Mammon respected that.

"Fine, but if you try to kill me, I'll—"

"You'll what?" Finn asked, practically smirking.

Mammon stole a move from the shifter and shrugged, letting his growl be heard, his eyes swirl with the power of his wolf. Letting his strength and intensity be a reminder to Finn. "Fuck if I know, but I'm sure you wouldn't like it."

Finn laughed as he climbed back into the fancy car,

even turning his back on Mammon in what could only be seen as an act of trust. Again, the man impressed Mammon. Something he didn't like having to admit.

Mammon followed Finn inside, ducking low through the door. The bench seat spread before him, wide and leather, with more space between the front and back than in an off-the-lot town car. This was a custom ride for sure and way nicer than anything Mammon had imagined. But he was still in a backseat, so leg room was an issue. Typical problem when you stood well over six feet tall.

"Nice ride," Mammon said once the driver closed the door behind him.

"It does the job." Finn rested against the seatback, turned just enough to watch Mammon angle his long legs into the space. The Dire shifted and twisted, but eventually gave up, kicking back against the door and stretching his legs across the middle of the floorboard. Right into Finn's space. The smaller shifter raised an eyebrow, but Mammon just grinned. He wanted Mammon in his car, this was what he got.

"So…talk, O'Rourke."

"So," Finn said, a slight smile curling up the corner of his mouth as he exaggerated the word back at Mammon. "You're mated to my best friend."

The Dire ignored the pang in his gut those words caused. Again. "You said that already."

"I did. I'm still surprised by it."

"Apparently."

Finn cocked his head, the first decidedly wolf move Mammon had ever seen the man make. "I never thought the fates would find a match for her."

The Dire shrugged, fighting the curiosity that statement evoked. "Never thought the fates would match me to a greedy criminal. They do like to play games, don't they?"

Finn growled low and deep, his eyes hard, his wolf

making itself known for sure. "Charmeine Byrne is not a criminal."

"But you are."

That shut him up.

Finn turned toward the window. "I do what I must to keep my family and friends safe."

"What's that supposed to mean?" Mammon struggled to hold in a snarl as his wolf suddenly raged in his mind. Keep them safe. Which meant they were unsafe at times, a thought that had his wolf lunging to the forefront, begging to get out. To protect. No one would touch his fated mate, even if he didn't want her by his side. Even if he walked away from her forever. No one would harm her. Ever.

Finn looked back at him, his eyes dark. Serious. "Have you ever heard of the Apex Hunters?"

Well now, that name was a blast from the past. "Sure. Mob types from Chicago. Grouped up in a bastardization of a pack and started killing shifters left and right to claim more territory and wipe out lines they felt were a threat to their reign. The NALB broke them apart almost a hundred years ago."

"Tried to." Finn sighed when Mammon didn't respond. "The NALB *tried* to break them apart. The plan didn't succeed."

That piqued more than just his interest in his mate and her safety. "Are you saying there's still a pack of Hunters out there?"

Finn huffed a laugh. "Pack? Not really, but there's a group of about ten, we think. Still out there, and still slaughtering entire bloodlines of shifters on some plan to rid the world of something only they know. Including the O'Rourkes." He stopped, staring at Mammon in a way that spoke volumes before quietly stating, "Including the last surviving member of the Byrne clan."

Byrne. Charmeine Byrne. Mammon's heart nearly stopped even as his wolf leaped to the front. He could practically feel his eyes swirl to the Dire Wolf silver, sense the way his ears would lift and prick as he took his animal form. But it wasn't the time to go wolf, not yet. There were things the man could do that the animal couldn't. Like call for backup.

"What are you doing?" Finn asked as Mammon yanked his phone out of his pocket.

"Ordering a pizza. What do you think I'm doing?"

Finn sat back, shaking his head almost sadly. "You can't tell anyone, Mammon. They'll make you a target if they found out. You don't understand their reach."

"Understand this—I work for Blasius Zenne, President of the NALB. He needs to be made aware of this immediately."

"I wouldn't do that." Finn grabbed Mammon's wrist, stopping him.

"Why the fuck not?"

Finn sighed, letting go of Mammon and sitting back against the seat once more. "You'll bring a war on you and your kin that can't be won."

Oh hell, that almost sounded like a challenge. Mammon didn't even attempt to hold back a smirk. "You have no idea who you're dealing with."

"Neither do you," Finn said, stiff and angry once more. "These shifters will slaughter anyone they see as standing in their way. They won't stop because some sanctions come down from a political figurehead."

"Blasius Zenne is much more than just a figurehead, and you really have *no idea* who or what you're dealing with here. But to err on the side of caution, I won't tell Blaze. Yet."

Keeping his eyes on Finn as much as he could, Mammon shot a quick text to Thaus. He could have chosen to notify Dante, Blasius' mate, or Phego, any other Dire Wolf, even.

But Thaus…well, he was a cut above the rest. More vicious, more violent when provoked. More set in a very black-and-white mentality of what was right and what was worthy of a death sentence. He was rage personified. If something wicked was coming for his mate, Thaus was exactly the man Mammon wanted fighting in his corner.

Once he hit send, Mammon leaned back against the seat once more. Eyeing Finn hard. Contemplating what he knew and what he *thought* he knew. "You do all this shit to protect your family?"

"If by shit you mean running a successful business by using the greed of the humans in the area against them, then yes. I do *this shit* to protect my family. And Charmeine."

"What about the hookers? This to protect them, too?"

That got a reaction. Finn looked positively livid. "We don't deal in sex, no matter what you think. Your mate would chop my balls off if I even brought that up as an option."

"She sounds pleasant." Mammon couldn't control the sarcastic sneer in his voice.

Finn just grinned, though. "Charmeine Byrne is amazing and strong, an Omega who truly lives up to the legend. She pulls people in, cares for them even to her own detriment. She loves the shifters we protect with her entire soul. Pleasant isn't a necessity in her world."

Mammon's jaw almost dropped. Charmeine was an Omega…he should have put that together. Until Bez had found Sariel, no Dire Wolf had been mated by the fates in hundreds upon hundreds of years. So color them all surprised when, a year later, Levi found his Amy. Both fated matches, both women Omega shewolves—ones surrounded by myths and legends of powers to hold packs together. Ones supposedly descended from the Dire Wolves that had brought him and his pack brothers into the world. She was part of his pack, even if she never accepted his claim on her as her mate.

Finn watched Mammon quietly, giving him a chance to collect his thoughts, he guessed. Not too much time, though.

"She's torn about you," Finn said finally, cocking his head when Mammon jerked back in surprise. "She's not heartless, and the mating pull affects her just as much as it does you. This situation is very confusing."

"I can understand that feeling."

"Yes, I bet you can." Finn tapped on the window separating the back from the front. "We'll head back to the parking lot now. Come by for dinner tomorrow."

The abruptness caused Mammon to blurt out a confused, "What?"

Finn raised a single eyebrow. "Dinner. It's a meal usually served in the evenings, sometimes called supper. As in to sup or to break bread. Let's say seven, does that work for you?"

"What? Why?"

"All these questions." Finn rolled his eyes. "The answer to what is a meal. The answer to why is to get to know Charmeine better and give her a chance to know you."

"Are you sure that's a good idea?"

Finn laughed. Guffawed, really. "Not at all. I have a feeling one of us will be crawling out of the dining room cupping our nuts before the meal is over. I'm sort of hoping it's you, to be honest."

Mammon huffed a laugh. "Gee, thanks."

Moments later, they came to a stop in the parking lot where the ride had begun. Mammon stepped out of the car, suddenly a little uncomfortable about what was to come. Nervous even. An alien sensation to the normally gruff shifter.

"So…" He took a deep breath, hanging on to the top of the door a little too tightly. "Tomorrow?"

"Seven. Be prompt. Charmeine hates tardiness." Finn

nodded once before Mammon closed the door and backed away. The car immediately took off, speeding through the night in a shower of dust and taillights.

Leaving Mammon feeling even more out of sorts.

"What the fuck just happened?"

The night didn't answer, though. Nothing did. So Mammon mounted his bike, giving himself a moment to sit and let his mind calm down. Dinner…with his mate and her BFF…both of whom he *should* despise. Totally not a big deal, right? Still, he grabbed his phone and sent a quick group text to Phego and Deus. He may have gone to Finn's house on his own the first night, but not this time. He had the element of surprise working for him then. This time, that advantage went to the O'Rourkes.

Mammon wouldn't be going in without backup.

The closets were too small, the lighting too fluorescent, and the paint an atrocious green color that Charmeine was sure went out of vogue in the late eighties. Still, she'd never been as thrilled as she was when she'd signed the contract to lease their temporary rescue space.

"Do you think we can fit another set of bunk beds in that back room?" Charmeine closed the door to one of the bathrooms that she'd paid to have scrubbed and revitalized for the new tenants and continued down the hallway, checking each room. Looking behind every door.

Ethan ran a finger over the floor plan, his meticulous notes penciled in for every room they'd investigated so far. "I believe so, yes. Though we don't have any more bunk beds. The order was for three sets."

Charmeine sighed and looked around again, picturing the old medical office suite as more than…well, an office suite. It wasn't too hard, especially considering it would be a temporary solution. Still, it wasn't perfect. Not yet. But it would do for their immediate needs.

This former office complex would be a new start for a lot of shifters, a safe place until Charmeine could sign on a real house. A true home. One with open land for their wolves to run and explore. Her wolf paced inside her head, nearly wild with the need to shift, to race for some sort of wilderness, to hunt and roam as she craved. Charmeine had to muzzle her, though. There was no time, and stretching Finn's security detail just so she could take a run was ridiculous. No. Her wolf would need to settle down for a few days longer. Maybe a week. Or two.

"Charmeine?"

She jerked back to attention, having lost herself to her inner beast for a moment. Ethan cocked his head, looking surprised by Charmeine's startled reaction.

"Right. Bunk beds. I'll call Finn," Charmeine said, shaking off the distraction of her irritated wolf. "Maybe he can help us until Al sends the trust disbursement."

Ethan practically choked on a harsh, sarcastic laugh. "Maybe? The man wears a Rolex."

"Don't be covetous, Ethan. Finn works hard and has to portray a certain image to be taken seriously. He's never turned me down when I needed a loan for the rescue, but I try not to rely on him anymore. I don't need to pile even more pressure on him because we weren't vigilant enough in New York to get out in time to bring the valuables."

Well, she brought the family valuables. Pictures and baubles she'd carefully unpacked from the linen bag she'd run with. Her mother's wedding ring, her father's cufflinks. But those treasures weren't worth cash, and right then, it was cash she needed.

"Of course. My apologies," Ethan said, though his tone was less than contrite and his eyes held more anger than not. "My apologies for assuming Finn's obvious wealth could be shared."

Charmeine could only sigh. Someday, Ethan would settle down and understand that riches weren't the answer to all things. Her family had been quite wealthy, and look where it had gotten them. The Apex Hunters hadn't cared about the money—they'd only cared about the blood.

Needing a distraction, Charmeine moved them along to the final room needing inspection. "How about we go up front and see if there's anything we can do to help? People will be arriving soon."

And indeed, they would. The few refugees who were sleeping on couches and floor pallets at Finn's house had begun repacking their belongings so they could move to the flat, boring building in the middle of more flat, boring buildings. It wasn't an ideal situation and not exactly the perfect place to put them all, but the options had been limited on such a tight time frame. Most places like this weren't zoned for overnight habitation, and most homes weren't big enough for the number of people Charmeine knew would be heading their way. This building—this huge, empty, sprawling complex—had once housed an ambulatory surgery center and a sleep clinic, so the entire unit was zoned to accommodate overnight stays. A lucky find for sure as they waited to find a true home.

Charmeine led Ethan to the first bathroom in the hall. Toilet, sink, small shower stall. Again, not ideal but workable.

"This one didn't get cleaned. I'll call the company first thing in the morning." Ethan scrunched his nose and regarded the room with distaste. Not that Charmeine blamed him.

"There are children moving in here tonight. That won't do." Charmeine looked over the grayed sink, the cobwebs hanging from the light fixture, and the toilet with mold in the bowl. This was the first bathroom off the entrance and would likely be a busy one. She couldn't leave the room as filthy as it was. "Hand me the gloves, please."

Ethan looked positively aghast but handed Charmeine a pair of plastic hospital-type gloves from the box they'd found in a cabinet when they first walked through the space. He had wanted to throw them away, but Charmeine had known they'd come in handy and made him carry a pair at all times as they set up the space. She'd been right.

"Can't we pay someone to do this?" Ethan stepped into the hall, leaving the door open.

"How can I ask the people who will be living here to clean up after themselves if I'm not willing to scrub, too?" Charmeine grabbed a scrub brush and some abrasive cleaner from the bag of supplies she'd been carrying with her and went to work.

Ethan could hate the menial labor all he wanted, but she relaxed as she cleaned. This was what she loved to do. Not scrubbing toilets necessarily, but taking care of people. The ones terrorized for no good reason by a band of militants trying to destroy something that didn't need to be destroyed. She'd worked for years to get to a point where the surviving victims trusted her, followed her guidance, and let her help them restart their lives. The Hunters still chased them, and sometimes they came awfully close to destroying what Charmeine had built, but she'd managed to stay one step ahead of them through bribes, spies, and sheer will to survive.

But this was it—the last time she'd be setting up a temporary space. Finn had been working hard to cement a steady income, and she would find the perfect place for the refugee families to create a pack home. They would come together to find safety in the number of members and the tight pack they'd form. And with Finn's network of muscle and his insiders all over the city, they'd know if any Hunters stepped foot in Fort Worth. They would live their lives in defiance of the Apex Hunters, and hopefully, Finn's men could begin hunting *them* down. Turn the tables. Destroy the handful who'd obliterated so many lives.

Her back ached and her arms burned as she scrubbed the filthy shower stall, but it was a good pain. The kind that came from working hard. The people who needed this rescue had traveled for days, looping and circling and taking back roads to stay off of the Hunters' grid. If those men, women, and children could put up with such lengthy drives, she could put up with a little soreness from cleaning.

So she scrubbed. And she damn near whistled while she worked.

Charmeine lumbered up the steps to Finn's house, hanging on to the handrail for the first time since she moved in. She ached all over, but the happiness burning bright within her made the pain worth the reward. Tonight, eight refugee shifters would sleep at the rescue. They had beds, new linens, clean facilities, and the start of a new life. The alarm Finn had installed would give them all an extra sense of security, something they needed after years of dealing with the Hunters. Altogether, it had been a phenomenal day. Exhausting, though. Charmeine was ready for a shower, a hot meal, and her bed. But when she finally made it to the top step and pushed open the door, she knew the night would not go as she'd hoped.

Her mate stood in the hallway, his back to her, unaware of her presence.

Tall and solid, the man seemed to take up much more space than the average person did. Mammon carried himself in such a way, with so much innate strength, as to seem to own the space around him simply by existing in it. Her eyes, so tired after her busy day, moved almost of their own accord, tracing the lines of his body. Following every curve and dip. She couldn't help herself; she simply had to look.

Muscled legs encased in dark slacks, a trim waist, ever widening frame leading up to broad shoulders. Arms like branches—thick and heavy. A cropped haircut, more military-like than most men wore. He exuded a level of danger that appealed to her in some way. Altogether, he reminded her of a soldier or a guard, a man out to protect something important, even in his dress pants and collared shirt. Someone on the defensive but ready to attack the unseen foe circling in the shadows. Appealing, but still a threat.

Especially to her.

Charmeine shoved the door closed, making sure it slammed into its frame. Might as well announce her presence. Mammon spun to face her, eyes going wide, literally looking her up and down. Inspecting her as she'd done to him only moments before. Perhaps he found her just as physically appealing, a thought that intrigued her. But the bold move on his part quickly forced her to go from interested to embarrassed. She had to be filthy from her day at the rescue.

She lifted a shaky hand and patted her hair, trying and probably failing to force the stray ones back into place. Tugged her shirt a little lower, hoping the bleach spots she knew were on the hem weren't too obvious. She fidgeted through many long, quiet seconds as Mammon simply stared…but then she stopped. Froze. Let her anger and resentment overthrow her need to please.

This man had no power over her.

No opinion from him mattered, no judgment ranked. She'd been doing what she loved all day, had helped numerous families, and would continue to help more in the coming weeks. Her being a filthy, smelly mess after a day of honest work should have been celebrated, not hidden.

"Do I need to call security?" Charmeine asked, tipping her chin and refusing to give him even the hint of a smile.

Mammon's eyebrow rose—just one—and his lips quirked up in a crooked sort of smile. One that sent a shiver down Charmeine's spine. But before he could answer— and certainly before Charmeine could throw herself at the big lug—Finn strolled out of the study. With two highball glasses in his hands and a rakish smile on his face, he looked his usual tidy, charming self. Charmeine could have smacked him.

"Ah, there you are. I was about to delay dinner to track you down if—" Finn paused, his brow furrowing as he looked her over. She stood a little taller, refusing to give in to the desire to huddle in a corner or run to her room. Why today? Why would he bring this stranger into his home, and why would he do it on the day she'd spent scrubbing toilets? Did the fates hate her that much?

She darted another glance at Mammon, her fated mate, who was still looking at her with that damnable, sexy smile. Yes—the fates definitely hated her *that* much.

"What the hell have you been up to?" Finn asked, finally moving again, if only to hand a drink to Mammon.

Charmeine didn't like being backed into a figurative corner. She looked over the two with a snooty sort of arrogance she'd learned to emulate from her nastier aunts and uncles. The benefits to being raised around wealth weren't all financial in nature.

"It's move-in time at the rescue. I spent my day cleaning and moving furniture so we were ready for the first residents." She glared, wishing she could growl at Finn, too. But she couldn't…wouldn't. That would be too far over the line in front of company. Still, she blew a stray hair out of her eyes and crossed her arms over her chest as she sent Finn a death stare. He needed to know she wasn't happy with him.

But if Finn picked up on her irritation, he didn't let on. In fact, his smile only grew. "Ah, I see. Well then. How about I take our new friend into the study for a drink while you get cleaned up. Dinner's in twenty minutes."

The dismissal rankled, and Charmeine bristled in response. "I'm not hungry."

Finn growled softly, throwing her the type of warning she knew better than to ignore. "You will not be rude to my guest, Charmeine. Clean up and join us for dinner."

A louder growl broke the stare-down between Finn and Charmeine. She shot a look to Mammon, the source of the threatening rumble. He was definitely glaring and almost snarling, but not at her. No, his menace was directed solely at Finn. Perhaps the man felt the need to come to her rescue, not that she needed him to. Finn would never hurt her. His demands were just him being bossy as usual. Still, having backup was sort of nice.

She looked back to Finn and raised her eyebrows. Waiting.

"Please," Finn said, gritting out the word with a stiff, plastic smile. "Get cleaned up and join us for dinner, please."

With a stiff curtsy and a glare, the likes of which most men would have cowered under, Charmeine flounced toward her room. Finn wanted to have dinner with the enemy? Fine. So be it. She'd join them as requested. But she'd come prepared.

ammon couldn't tear his gaze away from Charmeine as she walked away. The woman had shocked him, which was not an easy feat. She'd been so angry, so fierce and proud as she stood there, covered in dirt and far more mussed than she'd been the first time he saw her. Impressive, really. The woman *did not* back down from a fight, and she certainly wasn't the pampered princess he'd originally thought.

"There's a lot more to her than her ass," Finn said, his voice deep and dark in a way that screamed protective. Mammon drank down his whiskey and shrugged.

"It's not her ass that caught my eye." Which was mostly true. Her bravery and strength had definitely grabbed his attention, though Mammon couldn't deny she had a biteable ass. The woman filled out a pair of denim like no other. *Mercy.*

A quiet cough from Finn forced Mammon to refocus on the man beside him. That and the fact he knew Charmeine better than probably anyone else. Might as well take advantage. "Is she always so welcoming?"

Finn chuckled. "Oh, goodness, no. This is quite unusual. Normally, she's downright cranky."

Mammon blinked, speechless. Cranky? That *wasn't* cranky?

Meanwhile, Finn just smiled and nodded in the direction of the study. "How about we have those drinks now?"

"You're kidding, right?" Mammon asked as he followed Finn into the room he called a study. Looked sort of like a library to Mammon, but what did he know.

"Slightly." Finn grabbed Mammon's glass and moved to the bar, refilling both. "Charmeine does have her moods, though. Fair warning."

Mammon settled on a cushy leather chair in the room, nodding his thanks when Finn returned his drink to him. He sipped the amber liquid slowly, taking in the room around him. Bookshelves ran from floor to the vaulted ceilings on three walls, only a few windows taking up real estate otherwise reserved for books. On the fourth wall, the entryway dominated the vertical space, leaving very little room for anything else. Little, but not none. To one side, a picture hung all alone, a long, brass fixture mounted over it to bathe the image in golden light. An oil painting of two adults and two children.

"Your mate?" Mammon asked. The man did look an awful lot like Finn.

"No, actually. Those are my parents."

Huh. Mammon hadn't expected that answer. "So the children—"

"Charmeine and me. That was done not long after she came to live with us." Finn took a sip of his drink, staring at the painting with a small smile on his face. "Charmeine was so angry that day because she had to be dressed up.

She wanted to play outside in the woods, but my mother wouldn't let her for myriad reasons. She threw about twelve separate temper tantrums before she finally settled down and stood as my mother requested. Though, if you notice, she didn't smile. At all."

Mammon stared at the pale, unsmiling face. The artist had captured her well, making her look cherubic and thoughtful instead of angry, though there was a definite spark in her eyes. A sort of gleam that screamed of the trouble she could get into.

"She didn't want to wear the frilly dress?" Mammon remembered the night of the party—the silky material of her dress and the height of her heels. The sparkle of her jewelry under the chandeliers. He remembered every detail well. "That's surprising."

"It shouldn't be. She's still a shifter, an Omega shewolf at that. Her love of the outdoors rivals even the most wolf-centric shifters out there." Finn took another sip, finally tearing his eyes away from the painting. "You really should stop trying to put us in a box, Mammon. I'm not just a criminal, and Charmeine isn't just a rich socialite. She's a complex woman who happens to keep a particular persona in place for the public."

But Mammon couldn't resist one more hit. "So she's a good actress."

Finn growled, obviously pushed too far. "No, she's an amazing person with a huge heart who happens to be afraid of being taken advantage of, so she keeps most people at arm's length. There's a difference."

Mammon nodded, feeling chastised. And rightly so. But this place, this house, didn't fit with the stories Finn spun. Even with its modern lines, the mansion exuded a sense of wealth. Especially the study, a room filled with books from floor to ceiling. Books Mammon wondered about—did they ever actually get read? Were they beloved tomes with ragged pages and cracked spines or simply there for decoration? Mammon wasn't a money guy—he preferred relationships to partnerships, talking to spending—but even he knew the possible value of the books on the shelves. The number of libraries that would love to have them, the number of doors good stories opened for children and adults. Yet Finn hoarded them, seemingly as a show of the money he could spend. Something Mammon couldn't wrap his head around.

The band around Mammon's wrist vibrated, pulling him away from thoughts of money and waste. He tapped it twice before looking around the room. Seeking inspiration.

"So," Mammon started, reaching for any subject where he might find common ground with the wealthy crime boss. "Do you watch football?"

"I'm more of a baseball man myself."

Okay. Not that. "What about hockey?"

Finn's eyes practically lit up, and he leaned forward in his seat. "Oh, now that's an amazing sport. What's your favorite team?"

"The Red Wings."

"Oh." Finn frowned and sat back again, his expression hardening. "I'm a Blackhawks fan, myself."

"Ah." The silence reigned once more, the air growing thick and uncomfortable. Mammon tugged at his collar and gulped his whiskey, wishing for an escape. Shouldn't dinner be done already? Hadn't it been over the twenty minutes Finn had mentioned? And how long could it possibly take Charmeine to shower and change for a casual dinner? Mammon scowled internally—he didn't think he wanted to know that, to be honest.

"Well, at least we can agree on one thing as hockey fans," Finn said finally as he grinned over the rim of his glass.

Mammon searched his memory for one thing, one

positive attribute linking the Red Wings and the Blackhawks. And then he nodded. "Chris Chelios."

Finn raised his glass in a toast. "Chris Chelios."

"What about him?" Charmeine walked into the room as if she owned the world, which she may have for all Mammon knew.

She also sucked all the air right out of it.

Her hair hung in damp ringlets, her dirty jeans and shirt replaced with a light, simple dress that looked like it was made from the same fabric as some of his old T-shirts. His fingers itched to touch, to feel the fabric. To caress the curves underneath it and enjoy every ounce of softness her body and her clothes had to offer.

He stood up instead.

"There you are." Finn rose to his feet as well, approaching Charmeine to give her a kiss on the cheek. "You look lovely. Doesn't she look lovely, Mammon?"

Words. He needed words. Something agreeable even though he didn't think she looked lovely. Amazing…sexy… incredible…the most beautiful woman he'd ever seen, sure. Lovely…not so much.

Finn stared at him, waiting, the look in his eyes saying he knew exactly what he'd done by putting Mammon on the spot this way. The smiling fucker was going to die.

"Sure. Yes. Of course."

Charmeine's eyebrows rose, and her lips turned down. "I appreciate your enthusiastic response."

Oh, hell. That wasn't…*shit*. Not wanting her to think he found her lacking in any way, Mammon shot her a wicked smirk as he raised his glass. "You're stunning. I preferred the jeans is all."

Bingo. Charmeine's body relaxed, her anger apparently breaking. The way she looked at him, all bright eyes and ruddied cheeks, made Mammon want to kiss her. Want to lick the length of her neck and bury his teeth there. To claim her.

And wasn't that just a fucked-up thought to begin with? He was supposed to hate her, not want to throw her down and slide between those shapely legs. Shit, he was hard… again.

Finn's quiet chuckle—the one he tried to cover with a throat-clearing cough—cut the tension well, though, and distracted Mammon from the confusing situation happening in his pants. "So. Dinner?"

"Yes." Charmeine tossed her hair over her shoulder, looking quite possibly just as rattled as Mammon if the deep pink of her neck and cheeks was any indication. "Dinner would be a good idea."

Finn just chuckled again, the bastard. "Shall we move into the dining room, then?"

Mammon followed the other two through a doorway at the back of the room, feeling quite accomplished when his eyes stayed on Charmeine's back instead of her ass. Well, for most of the way. At least half. Maybe. Not that anyone could have blamed him. The thin fabric of her dress hugged every delectable curve and dip, showcased the long, lean muscles beneath her skin as the garment moved with her. It was hypnotizing. *Mercy, mercy, mercy.*

When he finally tore his eyes from that ass, Mammon checked out where they'd be eating. The dining room was about what he expected—big, with sleek furniture and cool colors on the walls. Perfectly in style with the rest of the house, even though the décor went against the classic exterior. Not that he was a master at design or anything, but those columns out front seemed to indicate grandeur.

The three moved to the huge table where only three places were set. One on the end—for Finn, he assumed— and one on either side.

How…normal.

Mammon followed Charmeine to her side of the table, leaning in to pull her chair out for her. Finn raised an eyebrow at the move, but Mammon ignored him. He could be a gentleman, for fuck's sake. As he pushed the chair back in, earning him a lovely smile from his even-more lovely mate, his wristband vibrated again. As soon as he made sure his mate was settled, he tapped the device twice. The signal to Deus that he was still alive and didn't need the team waiting a few blocks away to infiltrate the house.

That sort of technology was how Dires went in alone without going in alone.

"I hope you enjoy a good steak, Mammon." Finn smiled and draped his napkin on his lap.

"Yeah. Sure." Mammon followed the man's lead, placing his napkin across his lap before resting his forearms against the edge of the table. The few lessons about manners he'd learned over the years repeated in his head—don't slurp, don't put your elbows on the table, don't chew with your mouth open, napkin in lap, silverware used from outside in. So much information, it made his head hurt. How could a simple meal cause that much stress?

Finn, on the other hand, seemed completely calm and relaxed. "So, Charmeine, how was the rescue today? You said the families started moving in, correct?"

Charmeine glanced at Mammon before replying. "Perhaps this isn't the best time."

"No, I think this is the perfect time." Finn gave Mammon an appraising stare. "I think we can trust our friend here with the bare bones of your day."

That sounded almost ominous. "Trust me with what?"

But even though Mammon addressed Finn, it was Charmeine who answered. "The lives of children."

Well, that wasn't expected. Before he could reply,

though, a man walked into the room…a waiter, it seemed. At a private residence. He was in a whole new world.

Mammon had to sit back as a plate was slid in front of him. The scent of grilled steak almost made his mouth water, and yet he didn't make a move to eat it. Couldn't, no matter how good it smelled or how hungry he suddenly was. His wolf wouldn't allow it; not until his mate had been served.

A thought that rocked him right to the floor.

Fighting the mating instincts trying to force him to bend to their will, he grabbed his knife and fork and focused back in on the conversation. "You rescue children?"

"Families, really. Those affected by the Apex Hunters." Charmeine smiled at the server who brought her meal, then looked back to Mammon. Smile gone. Anxiety written across her pretty face. "I won't tell you where the rescue is."

"Understood, and I won't ask for that information." Mammon cut into his steak, his brow tightening as he frowned. "Are there many of them?"

"Children? No. Very few." Charmeine huffed an inelegant sort of snort. "The Hunters leave their prey with nothing. They kill anyone in their way, no matter the age. Whole families have been wiped out, entire packs."

Mammon set his silverware down, still concentrating on the woman across from him. "Entire packs going missing isn't something easy to hide. How did the NALB not know of this?"

"They're sneaky," Finn said, an angry rumble to his voice. "The Hunters don't hit established, well-known packs. They keep their focus on smaller ones, expansion groups or new packs formed from pack castoffs. Or, if they want to go bigger, they kill one at a time, making the pack suffer over months or even years."

Finn glanced at Charmeine, who seemed to be staring transfixed at her plate. Not moving. Barely breathing.

"Charmeine's mother and mine were best friends. Grew up almost as sisters." Finn cleared his throat, casting a worried look at the shewolf. "The Hunters hit the Byrne family hard. They killed Charmeine's parents first. Then they went after her cousins. Aunts and uncles. Every extended family member with the Byrne surname. When they were done, they tried coming after Charmeine, the last living Byrne, but she was too protected. They managed to take out my parents, though."

Charmeine finally raised her head, her eyes red and glassy but still defiant. She reached for Finn's hand, the two clinging to each other in a way that spoke of friendship and support. A way that clawed at Mammon's heart. The picture he had of them, his assumptions and ideas, shifted with every bit he learned, leaving him more adrift than ever.

Charmeine coughed and pulled her hand back, returning to her meal with practiced poise. An actress putting on a show. "They decimated my family over the course of two decades. When they came for Finn's parents, they promised to do the same to his. I won't stand for that."

The growl to her voice spoke to Mammon, called to the beast within him. Made him burn with fury and rage at the missed opportunities to help. To save shifters who needed saving.

The NALB and, by extension, the Dire Wolves, had failed their brethren.

"I'm sorry." Mammon tossed his napkin onto his plate, his appetite gone. "If we'd have known—"

Of course, Charmeine wouldn't miss that one. "*We* who?"

In timing that would never have been believed, the band on his wrist vibrated again. A check-in from Deus. His Dire Brothers doing their part to make sure he was safe. He tapped it twice almost out of habit, letting his thoughts cascade where they needed to go. Telling people he was a Dire Wolf was usually frowned upon. The seven of them protected their secret—the fact that any Dires were still alive—viciously and without fail. But Charmeine was his mate. She hadn't accepted him yet, but they were joined by fate. Just like Bez and Sariel, like Levi and Amy. She had the right to know. And Finn, apparently, would come along for the ride.

"I work for the president of the NALB in the role of Cleaner."

Finn sat back, eyeing Mammon hard. "You're a trained killer."

"No, I'm an investigator." He focused back on Charmeine, hoping she could see the difference. "I have killed, yes, but not without good reason."

But the disgust on her face spoke volumes. "What could be a good reason for murder?"

"We kill men like those in the Apex Hunters. Sick bastards who prey on their own and put every shifter at risk."

Charmeine frowned, but Finn seemed intrigued. "So you're a soldier for the NALB."

Mammon could only shrug. "Sort of. President Zenne has guards and police-style forces in place. My pack...we tend to be a bit more specialized."

The two stared at Mammon as if waiting for more. Not giving him anything to work with. So he shrugged again, and he kept his eyes on Charmeine's as he released his biggest secret.

"My brothers and I, we're Dire Wolves."

"Impossible," Finn said, a finality to his tone that brooked no room for argument. "The Dire Wolves have been extinct for ages."

Mammon knew the idea of a species long-thought to be extinct actually sitting at the guy's table would be a hard sell, but that didn't stop the growl that rumbled through him at being called a liar. "Or so you think."

"Or so the world knows. No Dire Wolves have been seen for centuries. Even the legends are mostly ignored these days." Finn positively glowered as he grabbed his highball glass once more. "This is absurd."

But it was Charmeine who surprised Mammon. "Let the man speak."

Mammon stood instead, dropping his wristband on the table and yanking his shirt over his head. Charmeine's eyes went wide, but he couldn't focus on that. Not yet or else he'd be hard all over again. That wouldn't be a good thing, especially not after he took off his belt and unzipped his pants.

"What are you doing?"

Charmeine's shock nearly made him laugh. "Probably not what you think."

He dropped his pants, giving his mate a chance to see just about every inch of him—which he noticed with glee that she took—before shifting to his wolf. If Finn knew the legends of the Dires, then he would know how to identify one. Their blocky heads, heavy jaws, and overall size were a good sign. But the killer, the absolute definition of a Dire Wolf identifier, were the spots that dotted their haunches and back. Ermine spots. Mammon's had always been particularly dark and spread out, more noticeable than most of the other guys. Those spots were like a calling card.

Without waiting for either shifter to give him an all clear, he stalked around the table, walking right up to the woman the fates chose as his. His wolf practically purred, desperate to see her through his own eyes, wanting so much to rub his scent all over her. He settled for plopping his head in her lap instead.

"Holy shit." Charmeine's hands shook as she ran her fingers along the edges of his ears. His ermine spots were darkest along the back of his head and neck, unlike the rest of his brothers, who tended to show more along their hips and backs. Charmeine seemed to trace every one, pressing into his fur in a way that sent him reeling. As much as he resisted the desire, hated feeling so out of control since the moment they met, he wanted her. And maybe he didn't hate that free fall as much as he thought. He liked being close to her, liked her smell and the silkiness of her skin. He liked her in that moment. Looking soft and sweet, inquisitive even. Her fingers in his fur, her scent filling his senses. Yeah, he liked her.

Still, he pulled himself away after only a minute or so and plodded back to his side of the table. All eyes remained on him when he shifted human. Leaving fur behind for skin… lots of very bare skin. He yanked on his pants for the sake of decency but left his shirt off. Left his napkin on the table, too. He'd just shifted in the middle of the dining room, and he needed a minute to resettle his wolf. Fuck manners.

"I didn't believe you," Charmeine said, her voice faint and almost regretful.

"No, you didn't. But that's okay. I've given you no reason to believe anything I say."

Finn sighed. "So secrets on all sides."

"Seems like it." Feeling a bit more in control, Mammon yanked his shirt over his head and took his seat with a sigh, examining what he knew about Charmeine from all angles. True, she seemed a bit uppity and high maintenance on the outside, but seeing her excitement over the rescue, her steadfast need to protect the people there… That showed a different side of her. A side he found extremely attractive. More so than he had thought possible. And she was in danger.

"I want to officially notify the NALB about all of this," Mammon said once he'd refastened his wristband. The last thing he needed was to miss a vibration and have a crew of Dire Wolves storming the O'Rourke mansion. "President Zenne needs to hear these stories to understand the situation. Your family, the others, the Apex Hunters' tactics, the information on the rescue effort…all of it."

"I still don't know if that's a good idea." Finn shook his head. "I don't see what they can do now that they couldn't do the first time they tried to end the Hunters."

Mammon shrugged, one side of his mouth kicking up in a smirk. "They can call in the Dire Wolves, and we'll take care of everything."

Finn still seemed wary, but Mammon was done trying to convince him. He knew exactly what he and his brothers were capable of—and how they would do anything necessary to protect one of their own. Charmeine being an Omega made her one of their own, even before the fates chose her as his mate.

"I'm not ready to antagonize the Hunters, not with so many refugees all on the road." Charmeine bit her lip, looking downright afraid as she glanced at Finn. Mammon couldn't have that. He leaned across the table, reaching for her. Ignoring her reluctance to take his hand.

"I won't sell you out. I promise. I only want to remove the threat so everyone can be safe once more."

But Charmeine didn't cave easily, not that he could blame her. "I don't trust you."

"I know, but we're your best shot at getting rid of the Apex Hunters once and for all. I'm—" he almost choked on the word, knowing they weren't yet at a place to accept their fates but needing to make himself clear "—your mate. The fates brought us together, and I won't betray them or you. You don't have to trust me yet, just put a little faith in the Dire Wolves. Let us help you. And in the end, you might learn to trust me just a little."

Charmeine shrugged a single shoulder and looked away. Ignoring him again. But that was okay. He had time. Not much, if these assholes really were after her, but some. Remove the threat, then deal with the woman. Sounded like a plan to him.

If only his wolf and his cock would get on the same page as his head.

Ten

harmeine needed to get her mate out of the house before she did something stupid like kill him…or kiss him. How on earth could someone so irritating be so hot? And why did Finn think bringing him into the house was a good idea?

"Another drink, Mammon?"

Damn him. Finn's words almost made her scream. Why was he not cooperating? Couldn't Finn see the stiffness to her shoulders? Couldn't he sense the tension?

Mammon…well, he certainly didn't seem to notice a damned thing. "Sure. I've got time."

Of course, he does.

"Charmeine?" Mammon's smooth voice saying her name did things to her. Things she wasn't ready to admit affected her. Things she liked.

Things that turned her words harsh and her tongue sharp. "What?"

Mammon's returning smile—the way one corner turned

up a little more than the other—fascinated her. She couldn't even make him mad, it seemed.

"Would you care for a drink?" Soft words, that smile, and a look that said he knew he was getting to her…and didn't care. Her mate was quickly finding every way under her skin.

And she had no idea how to stop him. "Martini, please."

"Martini for the lady." Finn headed for the bar in the corner, leaving Mammon and Charmeine in an awkward, tension-filled silence. The sort of tension that left her practically panting. What *was* this nonsense and why couldn't she control herself?

But before Finn could pour a single drink, one of his guards came hurrying into the room. "Sir, a moment."

Finn sighed, meeting Charmeine's eyes for a long, meaningful look. "I need to deal with something."

Of course, he did, which meant she would be left alone with her mate. Heaven help them both.

The smile Charmeine pasted on her face was about as fake as they came, but the best she could do considering the way her knees were practically shaking under her skirt. "Certainly. Don't let us hold you up."

Finn's irritated expression told her she'd hit a nerve, though that didn't stop him from walking out of the room. Always working. Always hustling. And now he'd left her alone with a man she didn't trust. One who sparked something hot and needy within her. Wonderful.

"Good thing I know my way around a bar." Mammon stepped in to finish Finn's job, pouring liquor into glasses, even humming while he did so. An odd thing for a man who looked as if he could tear your arm off without thinking about it. Charmeine watched him, completely fascinated by the way his muscles made his shirt pull tight when he lifted his arms. The way his pants hugged his hips and thighs. The way the fabric slid over every sensual, strong inch of him.

"Dirty?"

Charmeine jerked to attention, ripping her eyes away from the muscles corded along his arm and meeting his gaze. A mistake, for sure. Those dark eyes saw too much.

"Excuse me?"

Oh, that smirk. That naughty smirk made her breath catch and her heart fly. Mammon was deadly in so many ways. "Do you want it dirty? The martini?"

"Yes, I do, though I don't care for innuendo."

"I'm just talking about a drink, Charmeine. Nothing more, nothing less." He turned back to the bar, giving her the opportunity to watch him in action again. To fight the need within that made her want to run her hands over every inch of muscle he carried, to know what it felt like. What it tasted like.

She needed to get away from him before she did something stupid.

Turning, she forced herself to peruse the shelves instead of the man across the room. Books were safe, solid. Sure. Mammon was…dangerous. Wild. The unknown. She should focus on the books.

But Mammon threw that option out the window when he walked over to hand her a martini glass with six olives in it. "Dirty. Just the way you like it."

Her wolf practically purred, the hussy. "Thank you."

The glass felt cold to the touch, but his fingers were warm. Hot even as they brushed against hers. As they stayed in contact for far longer than necessary. And his eyes, those dark, deep eyes, sparked with something luminescent. Something bright and ethereal. Something wild. She held her breath, waiting for him to break contact, unable to do so herself. The scent of him, the warmth, was more than she could handle. More than she could refuse.

But there was no way she would admit that.

"So," Mammon said when he finally—*finally*—released her from his witchcraft touch. He drawled the word, lips and tongue and voice turning each letter into something more, something sensual. "Nice books."

Spell broken by books, just as she'd hoped. It took effort to breathe, to smile, but she had a focal point now. The books. "They are, aren't they? Finn has dragged them across the country and back several times. He refuses to live without them."

Mammon approached a shelf and ran his fingers over the spines. A simple touch, but one that seemed almost gentle. Loving. The sign of someone who enjoyed slipping inside the pages. *"It is what you read when you don't have to that determines what you will be when you can't help it."*

Charmeine cocked her head, appraising him. Completely unable to hide her surprise. "Oscar Wilde."

Mammon smiled before taking a book off the shelf. "Yes, and quite accurate, I believe."

Unable to resist her pull to him, she stepped closer. Wanting to see which book he'd chosen. Wanting to breathe in that warm, oaky scent some more. "And how does Finn do in terms of what he chooses to read?"

Mammon glanced around the room, his eyes stopping now and again on different bookcases. "Classic literature, historical biographies, war memoirs, and nonfiction business titles…all things I expected. But those—" He closed the book and returned it to the shelf before striding across the room to the far corner, the shelves tucked beside the bar where he'd made their drinks. Charmeine knew where he was headed before he got there, and she felt no need to follow. Instead, she sat on one of the leather couches, sipping her martini and waiting for the question she knew was coming.

"Did you know Finn was a fan of Judy Bloom?"

Her laugh was inelegant at best, an almost cackle at worst. "Those are mine, of course."

He smiled over his shoulder before grabbing one off the shelf. "*Blubber.*"

"A tale of bullying."

"Yes, I know." He flipped through the pages, frowning. "And yet, no resolution comes. The children aren't punished for being so cruel to one of the others, the friendships aren't redeemed, and the main character is still sort of…well, bratty."

It took Charmeine a long handful of seconds to find her voice. "You've read *Blubber*?"

Mammon shrugged, as if his knowing the story details of *Blubber*—having obviously read it enough to remember key bits—wasn't one of the most attractive things a man had ever admitted to.

"I read a lot. Mostly fiction, though some nonfiction if it strikes my fancy. Young adult novels often deal with tough subjects, like bullying. You can't understand the human if you don't understand how their experiences have formed their perceptions." He set the book back on the shelf carefully, as if it had value beyond the paper it was made of. Something so oddly attractive, she nearly purred.

"What else do you read?" Mammon asked as he sat beside her. Not too close, though—giving her room to breathe. To keep her from feeling crowded. A fact she hadn't expected. Though she really hadn't expected anything about this night, especially how much her body craved his touch.

"Anything." Charmeine refused to give in, sitting farther back in the corner to put more space between them. "Newspapers, magazines, literary fiction, romance, encyclopedias."

Mammon chuckled. "Encyclopedias? You still have those?"

"Of course." She smiled, unable to help herself. "Because of the threats around us, we were stuck inside a lot as children. Finn and I spent a good deal of time in studies like this one with his father."

"So your love of reading comes from his dad?"

Charmeine tucked her legs beneath her. "No, not necessarily. My parents read to me as well, though I'm not sure even their influence lasted. I simply needed to escape from the hell my life became after their murders, and books gave me that."

Mammon growled low and deep, an unhuman sound. One that evoked fear instead of arousal. Mating haze thrown off, her instincts came down to fight or flight. Something she was much more accustomed to.

Charmeine was up and moving before she could think, trying to run. To escape his presence. God, he was an animal, more so than the other shifters she knew. More dangerous. To her, especially.

"Charmeine, wait."

"You don't need to growl at me," she said, glaring as he rose to his feet. Still backing away.

"I wasn't growling *at you*. I was growling because of the situation you don't deserve to be in."

But her doubt remained high, her need to run strong. Not enough to make her feet actually head for the hallway, but enough to inch backward as he came closer. "You don't need to do that, either. I'd rather you controlled yourself in this house."

Mammon stopped, his eyes turning darker, his head cocking. More animal-looking than ever. More frightening. "You want to see me controlled?"

A punch to the chest, those words. One that made her shake. Made her shiver at their tone. "No, I...I want you to behave as a person should."

"I'm not a person, Charmeine." He stepped closer. Slowly. Looking more like a predator with every inch he gained. "I'm a wolf, and a damn strong one. A Dire. I can tell you deny your animal side, but I refuse to. My inner wolf is happy, is a true partner in my life. And we can tell that the poor beast inside you is locked up so tight, you barely feel her."

Charmeine's wolf stayed silent, watching from within her. Not fighting back against the words she knew—or hoped—were untrue. "You know nothing."

"Then tell me."

But her heart had hardened, her mind closing him out. "No."

"Why not?"

"Because, I don't—" She couldn't say it. Wanted to, needed to let him know she didn't trust him, but the words wouldn't come.

"You don't what?" Mammon asked, pushing her. Refusing to let up. "Tell me."

An order. And there it was. The anger, the wall keeping her from letting him in. "No."

Mammon sighed, shaking his head before pinning her with his glare. "Are you always such a brat?"

"Are you always such a cretin?"

Mammon growled again, stalking toward her. Charmeine took an involuntary step back. He was pushing her, hunting her, and while this side of him brought back all those needing, wanting feelings of desire he'd caused earlier in the evening, she wasn't going to let him rule her. Wasn't going to give in to his…anything.

"I know you feel what I feel, Charmeine."

Her back hit the bookshelf. Trapped. She swallowed hard and held her ground, refusing to surrender to him. "Hardly. Curious, maybe, as one might be when they come upon a strange insect or animal. A fuzzy squirrel, perhaps."

His growl made her knees quiver, but she locked them into place. "Did you just call me a squirrel?"

"No." Breathy, no fire behind that word. She tried harder. "I compared you to one, but technically, I didn't call you one."

His hands, those huge, strong hands, landed on either side of her shoulders as he leaned in. She was trapped, boxed, caged by the sheer thickness of him. And God save her, she liked it more than she feared it.

"You put up a good front, Char. But you forgot one key piece of information I have against you."

"What information did I forget?" How could she speak? How could she open her mouth and not just groan? She had no idea. The man overpowered her without a touch, dominated without intention. He inched closer, his body brushing hers. She could feel the warmth, could practically taste him on the air. Her quivers traveled up and down her body, making her shake with need. With desire. Every inch of her in tune to every inch of him. Every thought completely dialed in to what he was doing or saying. There was no escaping his presence.

Mammon leaned in farther, running his nose over her cheek to her ear. Barely a brush of skin, but enough to make her bite back a moan. To make her practically dissolve into a puddle of want and craving. To make her—

"I can smell you."

It took Charmeine a moment to decipher his words, but when she did, her temper flared hotter than the sun. Spell broken once more. "How dare you be so crass?"

"How dare you not ask for what you need?"

"You have no idea what I need." She pushed his shoulder, trying to move him. A fruitless effort and one that worked against her. He grabbed her wrist, held it, kept a physical contact that only made her body itch for more. Made her heart jump and her breath catch. Traitorous hormones.

"I know exactly what you need," he murmured, his voice rough, his growl undeniable. "What I don't know is why you won't give in and let yourself have it. Let go and take what you want, baby." This time, he pushed her back against the shelves. Trapping her. Pressed the two of them together from shoulder to waist. But that wasn't enough. Not for her, no. She rocked her hips forward, soft and subtle. Teasing… curious. But there was no soft or subtle when it came to the man chosen as her mate. The hardness, the ridge of steel in his pants screamed to her. She sought more contact. Wanting to understand the girth of him, the desire he obviously experienced around her.

He moaned at the contact, and her eyes fluttered, the two moving in concert. Tiny brushes, a little added pressure here and there. A rough, almost-dry hump while standing up against the bookshelves in the study, mostly clothed, too pissed at each other to give in and get what they needed.

Until he spoke again.

"No one has to know that I get you wet simply by breathing the same air." He growled low, making her entire body quake. "You think I'm any less immune to you? Jesus, woman. I'm hard every second around you."

She mashed their lips together in a kiss just this side of painful. She hated him and his filthy mouth, but damn did the man know how to kiss. Tongues sliding, breaths gasping, they kissed like a couple going down in flames. As if they'd never meet like this again, so that kiss was their one shot. And maybe it was, but at that moment, Charmeine couldn't have stopped to save her life.

As the kiss turned harsher, positively brutal, Mammon grabbed her by the back of the thighs and lifted her right off the ground before using his body to press her against the shelves. A wiggle, a squeeze, and she had him exactly where she wanted. So hard for her, so perfect as the head of him rubbed against the parts of her screaming for his attention. She wanted him…no kidding, joking, or lying. She wanted him naked, wanted to ride him until his entire body bowed beneath her, wanted to see this tough man crumble. But the stubborn streak that had kept her alive for so many years wasn't ready to break.

Instead, she rocked her hips against his. Intentionally and with a rhythm that couldn't be ignored. Mammon, bless him, mimicked her motions. Lifting her with each press. Dragging that erection against her clitoris with every retreat. Driving her wild for him.

"Make me come," she gasped as she clutched at his shoulders.

"Demanding little thing aren't you?" He grunted, probably reacting to her nails embedding themselves in his skin as she clawed at him. Not that she cared. She scratched harder, clutched him tighter as he rocked more earnestly. Rolling his hips in the most perfect way. Fuck, the man could move. And still he held her, lifted her, acted as if her weight was nothing. And wasn't that just the hottest thing ever?

She gasped as he hit a spot so good, it made her eyes roll back. Mammon chuckled in response, angling to move in the same way.

"That it?" he asked, his breath coming faster and his voice deliciously dark.

"Just…don't stop."

"Not even if you begged."

Charmeine sank her nails deep into his shoulder, unable to resist. "I'd never beg."

"Oh, baby. I'll definitely make you beg at some point." Mammon's growl was the only warning she had before he lifted her, practically tossing her in the air. His arms cradled her legs, his elbows holding her knees.

"You stopped." She almost grinned as he huffed and pressed himself against her once more.

"I readjusted for a better experience. There's a difference."

She shrugged, trying hard to play it casual. Trying not to show him how desperate she was for more. "Looked like stopping to me."

He thrust along her, a single, strong push. The head of his dick rubbing the entire length of her pussy. Teasing her. "Does this feel like stopping?"

Charmeine could only shake her head, the pleasure too much to form words. She was spread for him, a lewd position for sure, but the increased sensations were worth it. Her being so open, so exposed, her dress hiked up to reveal her soaked pink panties, her pussy practically on display, left her more available and sensitive. Gave him more room to tease her with every roll forward. And he took advantage. Of course, he did. Rocking his hips, thrusting, using his position to spread her wider so he could tease her entrance. She had no idea how he was so flexible, so in tune to what she craved, but she liked it. She liked it enough that her entire body buzzed with the need to come, with the draw to let go and give in to her release.

So she did.

As he grunted and growled, she gasped. A simple noise, quiet and refined, but he picked up on the cue. He pushed harder, pressed closer, leading her through an intense orgasm that had her clutching him to her. Had her shaking and shivering all over. Had her biting down on his neck as if she were accepting the mating.

And Mammon, he never stopped, never paused. He let her have her moment, let her do what she needed. Even with her teeth against his flesh, he didn't pause. And though she didn't break the skin, she knew he wouldn't have stopped if she had. Didn't know how, but she felt it. Was certain. The man was practically a sex machine with the amount of focus he kept on her.

But as she came back to herself, as she sagged in his arms, she felt him. Hard. Needing.

Charmeine tossed her head back against the shelves, meeting Mammon's eyes for the first time since their kiss. "You—"

He shook his head. "Not about me."

She leaned forward, licking his bottom lip, a single moment of sweetness in all the not-so-sweet. "But you're hard."

He chuckled, letting her legs drop but still holding her up. "Nice of you to notice. But it's okay. I'd rather not come in my pants."

Charmeine cocked her head, her brow pulling down. Mammon responded to her quizzical look with an arrogant smirk. As expected.

"Now, if you'd like me to take them off…"

Charmeine rolled her eyes and pushed him away. Her legs wobbled at first, but she held it together. Kept putting one foot in front of the other even as she gripped Mammon's hand and tugged him behind her.

"I refuse to owe you."

"Hey." Mammon stopped her, forcing her to look his way. "There's no owing here. You do whatever you're comfortable with, and I'll deal with me. I don't want you to fuck me just because you think you carry some debt for what I just did."

"Oh, Mammon. Haven't you figured it out yet? I always do exactly what I want." She pushed him back, watching with glee as he fell onto the couch. As that big, bad man collapsed because she wanted him to. Eyes locked on his, she pulled up the skirt of her dress and hooked her thumbs in her panties.

"What about Finn?" Mammon asked, looking as if Finn was really the last thing on his mind.

"Finn won't be back. The staff won't bother us either unless I call for them. And I don't plan on calling for them." Pink silk and lace dragged against her skin as she pulled her panties down. Mammon stared, transfixed, his eyes following the scrap of material as she let it fall to the floor then kicked it to the side.

"What are you up to, Char?"

"No one calls me Char."

"I do."

"I've noticed." Charmeine leaned over him, unfastening his belt and pants. Mammon grunted but lifted his hips, allowing her to pull layers of fabric down his legs. Commando…of course.

"Do you like it?"

It took Charmeine a moment to realize he was talking about the nickname and not his erection.

"No." A lie, really. She liked it; she also liked what she saw. Long and thick, his erection stood proudly. God, she wanted to feel that inside of her, wanted to know how much it would fill her, stretch her. How tight everything would get when she came around it. But this wasn't the time.

"Then I'll keep doing it," Mammon said, giving her that wicked smirk again.

There was something about his brashness, his crude words and his rough actions, that ramped up her desire to lead him. To overpower him. And what better way to overpower a man than to control him through this act. She wanted to take him in, decide how far and fast he could fuck her mouth, and make him come on her tongue. She needed it. She was practically starving for him. But she wasn't ready to give without getting as well.

"You call me Char, and I might not answer."

"Sure you will. You like me too much not to."

"Lies." Charmeine raised an eyebrow then pulled her skirt to her waist. Mammon's eyes dropped, his growl coming hard and fast as he took her in again. Though Charmeine was more fascinated by his erection, which bobbed slightly in response to her nakedness. Apparently, she wasn't the only one who liked what they saw.

She lifted her leg over his chest, straddling him as she faced his feet. "I want to come again, and I'm going to make you come as well."

He gripped her hips, pulling her ass cheeks apart, rubbing her. "You like being in charge, don't you?"

Charmeine looked over her shoulder and smiled. "I told you, I always do what I want. And right now, I want to come with your tongue on my pussy."

Without a moment of hesitation, she bent over and took his weighty erection in her mouth. No introductory licks or teasing touches. No, the man needed to come. His cock dripped with desire, probably hurting with the level of his need. As much as she hated him—and she was pretty sure she still hated him, at least in her mind—she wanted him to find his release. And she wanted to give it to him…with her mouth.

Mammon, bless him, jerked and groaned as she sucked him down. "Holy shit."

Charmeine didn't pause, though. She sucked and licked and pulled him all the way inside. One hand on his thigh for balance, the other between his legs as she fondled his heavy sac, she gave him as much as she could. And he liked it. He thrust and growled, cursing softly behind her.

And then his tongue was on her clit and his lips were sucking her sensitive flesh. She almost stopped her attention, almost gave in to the desire to let him take care of her and focus on her own pleasure. But she wanted to taste him, needed it. Craved his release more than her own.

His mouth was brutal, rough and aggressive, just like him. His fingers, blunt and thick, pushed inside her as he lapped at her. She moaned around him at the intrusion, earning a bigger thrust of those fingers and a scrape of his teeth against her clit. Damn, the man was talented.

"Char," he gasped, giving her the warning his body already had. She hadn't failed to notice the way his legs shook or how hard the muscles in his abdomen had become as she'd worked him. He was close, but so was she. Ignoring his plea, she moaned again and kept up with her motions, increasing her speed. Mammon pulled his fingers away but went back to work with his mouth, running his tongue along the length of her opening before pushing inside. Charmeine shivered, so very close again. Ready to fall but determined to take him with her.

Hips rocking, legs shaking, Charmeine kept pushing even as she wanted to break. His tongue felt so good against her, his mouth so hot. But not yet. She concentrated on the feel of him in her mouth instead. The weight of him. The taste. But when he growled against her, when his lips vibrated and his hips thrust up and he finally fell, she couldn't hold back.

Shivering, shaking, she came as he did. She barely remembered to swallow, her mind so caught on her own pleasure. On the shock waves rolling through her.

It took far longer to regain her composure than she'd hoped. The warmth of his body against hers, the feel of his hands caressing her back, all led her to fall into a comfortable sort of haze. But eventually, she remembered. The families that had been torn apart, the packs that had been destroyed, the lives that had been ended because someone trusted an outsider. There were children under her care, shifters young and old who needed her to stay on her guard. She could not fall for a charming man who may not be who he said he was. Eventually, she remembered who she needed to be and how she shouldn't trust him. And so, as heartbreaking and physically agonizing as it was to do, she pulled her figurative mask back into place. And she crawled off him.

"Where you going?" His words were slightly slurred, a happy sort of drawl to them. The kind that spoke of sleep, of affection. Of intimacy and trust. All things she couldn't give him.

"I need a shower." She lifted her chin, readying herself for the fight. Knowing he wouldn't like her next words. Knowing she wouldn't, either. In fact, hating herself for even saying them but picturing all the refugees she'd helped over the years, their faces stained with tears from night terrors. The fear they carried with them every single day. She had to. Her life was not just about her. "I think you'd better go."

His face. She couldn't look at it, couldn't meet his pained eyes. Couldn't even glance his way for fear of tearing up. "Char."

A shiver screamed up her spine when he spoke that one word, one she forced her body to ignore. "My name is Charmeine."

Mammon's hurt turned to anger quicker than she expected. "So this is it? You get off and kick me out without even a postcoital snuggle?"

The words cut, because deep down, she wanted to snuggle with him for days. She wanted to lie in his arms and imagine she was safe. But it wasn't safety she saw when she closed her eyes and tried to imagine her future. It was blood—on her shoes, on the wood floors, on her father's old desk. Blood everywhere. Something she couldn't allow to happen again. She wanted more things than she could ever have, but most of all, she wanted to keep her wards safe and secure. She wanted them to live a life very much unlike her own.

So she tugged down her dress and grabbed her panties, making sure to leave no trace behind of what they'd done.

"I don't snuggle."

Mammon snorted a sarcastic half laugh. "You think a blow job is somehow less intimate than a cuddle?"

"Sex is physical, not emotional. Now, cuddling?" She leaned over him, looking him right in the eye. Locking her emotions behind the tallest, thickest wall she had. "Being naked together, really naked, as in more than just skin on skin, is true intimacy. That's personal." She stood and ran a hand over her hair to smooth it. "You've had a piece of my body. That doesn't mean I've given you any of my heart."

But Mammon's temper didn't flare as she'd expected. Instead, he sagged into the couch, watching her. Looking almost…challenging.

"How do I earn it?"

His honest question stopped her in her tracks. Her answer something automatic and vague. "I have to trust you first."

She should have known Mammon wouldn't let her get away with that, though. He reached for her, his flinch obvious when she jerked away.

"How do I get you to trust me?"

And wasn't that the question? She very well might have wanted to trust so she could learn more about him, but the threat, the fear, was stronger than her curiosity, and she wasn't sure she could move past that. Wasn't sure she should even try.

"I don't know." Charmeine didn't even give him a glance as she walked toward the doorway. "I don't know if I *can* trust anymore."

Eleven

ammon knew someone would be in his apartment long before he approached the door, which certainly didn't help buoy his mood any. He'd been hoping for some time alone to get his thoughts in order, but nope. Wouldn't be happening. The black Suburban and the Jeep in the lot gave his Dire brothers away. Apparently, he would have a debriefing before he could think about his mate, her situation, and how he had no idea if she'd ever truly accept him. Now that he actually wanted her to.

Matings were too complicated sometimes.

Without thinking it over, he grabbed his phone and typed a quick message to Charmeine. She'd probably be a little shocked that he knew her cell number, but he didn't care. Being a Dire Wolf came with privileges, one of them being having Deus to hack into various databases to find the information they needed. And right then, he needed to talk to his mate.

I won't stop trying to earn your trust, just so you know.

Prepare to be courted.

Her response came before he'd finished climbing the stairs to his level of the building.

Who is this? And no one says courting anymore. You should try to keep up with the times.

Feisty. He liked it. And he was damn sure she knew exactly who was texting her.

And you should try to get some sleep. Maybe read a book. If you grabbed Blubber *off the shelf, I bet it'd still smell like me.*

He almost laughed. She'd definitely have something to say about that. But before he could deal with her, though, he needed to handle whatever was waiting for him in his apartment. Fuck, what a long night.

"Lucy, I'm home." Mammon walked inside and closed the door behind him, eyeing the three Dires sitting around his tiny efficiency. Dwarfing it, really, not that the place needed any help in that department. He would have said the Dires would be a better fit in the extra-large dining room at the O'Rourke estate, but that would be a lie. They wouldn't fit there either in their dark jeans and combat boots. No, these boys would fit best in some dark, smoky bar where dart boards, fried foods, and cold beers were the selling points of the night. Far removed from the steel and stone of the O'Rourke mansion. Not a one of them belonged there.

And yet, Mammon ached to go back…to be with his mate. Not his brothers, who seemed to think they owned his space.

Bez was all leaned back in his chair, balancing on just the back two legs, scowling and probably trying to seem dangerous. Both habits Sariel had yet to break him of. Thaus, on the other hand, had his head back and his eyes closed. The bastard looked as if he was napping.

But it was Phego, sitting board straight and looking

ready to flay the skin from Mammon's hide, who caught his attention.

"You got a problem?"

"Just you, man," Phego said, his growl solid and steady. A definite warning.

Mammon chose to ignore that fact. Instead, he grabbed the last chair and spun it around before straddling it. "So what's the situation?"

Bez cocked his head in a very predatory sort of way, snarling something fierce. "Are those claw marks on your neck? Why didn't you let us know you were in trouble? Deus. Your piece-of-shit watch-thing didn't work."

"Not possible," Deus said, his voice coming from the phone leaning against the microwave on the counter. "My shit works. I show no record of a missed double-tap."

As hard as he tried, Mammon just couldn't hold back a satisfied grin at the thought of Charmeine's marks on his body and his skills in the secret-agent department. How he'd kept track of the vibrations and tapping during that whole dry-hump-sixty-nine fiasco was beyond him. "I'm sure the wristband would have worked if I'd called for help."

Thaus growled, apparently awake. "The rules were clear. You call for help if you ran into trouble of any kind."

"No, I was to call for help if I had trouble with Finn or his guys. I had no trouble *with them*." Mammon sighed, not wanting to get into the details but knowing he had a team to account to. "The scratches aren't from fighting."

The guys fell silent, considering, but then Bez, of all people, chuckled. "Well, you *are* mates."

Mammon didn't like that statement. "What's that supposed to mean?"

Bez shrugged and smiled. *Smiled.* A shocking development, really, seeing as how Mammon couldn't remember the man smiling in at least two hundred years.

But there he sat, shorn head, pale eyes, and all…grinning like a motherfucker.

"When I was with Sariel at the safe house, I had an enemy team less than thirty minutes out, and I still couldn't resist the mating pull."

"Levi had Amy in the shower thirty minutes after killing that fucking shifter who kidnapped her." Thaus finally opened his eyes, peering at Mammon. "We all heard that shit."

Deus sighed loud enough to hear the sound through the phone. "I am so thankful for the internet right now."

"Enough of this." Phego waved a hand, indicating that conversation was over. "We can't be so careless with time simply because of our desires. Even mates can be dangerous if they're embedded in the wrong team. We should trust no one until we figure out what's happening."

Phego's words slammed into Mammon in a way he hadn't expected. He sounded so much like Charmeine, both with trust issues that ran deep enough to make them push away people who might be able to help them. Mammon understood Phego's issues, having been close to the man for centuries at that point. But Charmeine… He was only beginning to see how much of a job earning her trust was going to be.

"Phego is right," Deus said. "Trust no one, especially not a woman willing to have sex with Mammon. Have you seen him eat? He's practically an animal."

"Y'all are funny as shit, but I managed to eat without making a spectacle of myself tonight. So fuck off." Mammon stood and headed for his bathroom at the back of the apartment, leaving his brothers to razz him behind his back. Before he could reach the door, though, his phone buzzed with a message from Charmeine.

I don't think I'll ever look at Blubber *the same way again.*

You've ruined it for me.

Mammon couldn't hold back his smile.

I've made it better. Imagine how wet you'll be the next time you reach for that paperback.

Crass.

Honest. Go to bed, Char, before I ruin more of your favorite books.

Mammon pocketed the device and looked up, meeting the eyes of one pissed-off looking Phego. The shifter leaned against the opposite wall, legs crossed at the ankle.

"What's up?" Mammon asked.

"She doesn't trust you."

Mammon bit back the *no shit* answer on the tip of his tongue. "She doesn't trust anyone."

"Until she does, you're in danger every time you're around her."

"I think you're overreacting," Mammon said, very nearly rolling his eyes.

"And I think you're being careless. She won't hesitate to sell your soul to the devil if she feels threatened in any way, and you'll take us all down with you." Phego dropped his voice. "I know people like her…I've *been* people like her. You won't walk away from that fight."

"Fine," Mammon said with a growl, too tired to fight about it. "So how do I convince her she can trust me?"

"You don't."

"Well, you're a helpful SOB."

"You can't convince someone to trust you, especially not someone with walls as high as hers are. You can only act in a way that builds trust slowly. That proves who you are."

Mammon ran a hand over his face, his chest tightening as the words of his brother hit home. "I never thought I'd need to bend myself into a pretzel just to get my mate to like me."

"Oh, I'm sure she likes you. Those claw marks are proof of that."

"Being turned on by me and liking me are two different things."

Phego shrugged. "Maybe. Maybe not. But she trusted you enough in that moment to be alone with you, to let her guard down and share a physical intimacy."

But it wasn't…she'd made sure of it. "She said sex wasn't intimate."

The corner of Phego's mouth twitched, a goddamned emotional outburst from the stoic shifter. "She's a harder nut to crack than I thought. I'm almost impressed with the arrogance of that comment."

"Gee, thanks."

But Phego didn't back down. "Deus gave us all the details he could find after you sent Thaus that bullshit text last night. You're talking about a woman whose family was murdered in front of her, who's been hunted for years by a group of sick fucks bent on destroying her. She's not some broken damsel in distress. She's a fucking warrior."

Mammon sagged against the wall, staring at the floor. "You have no idea, man."

"That's where you're wrong." Phego's growl deepened, his eyes sparking silver as he crept closer. "Charmeine Byrne is the most deadly thing you've ever run into because of your bond to her. You'll protect her to your death and do anything she wants you to without question. It's the pull of the mating, I get that, but you still need to let us, your brothers, know what's going on so you don't walk into some sort of ambush with these Hunters. Or a setup."

"She wouldn't do that."

"No? She's already got you so wrapped up in her puss—"

The words ended in a hiss as Mammon grabbed Phego by the throat and yanked him off his feet. "Don't. She's my fucking mate, not just some chick hanging around. You mind your fucking mouth about her."

Phego kicked, his claws digging deep into Mammon's hands, but it was no use. Mammon wasn't letting go until he'd made his point. His inner wolf wouldn't let him. It took a few seconds, but Phego finally jerked a nod. Accepting. Surrendering.

With nothing more than a growl, Mammon dropped his brother and took a step back. His wolf settled once more, still ready to attack the man he saw as a brother if he opened his mouth again. Over Phego's shoulder, Mammon could see Bez and Thaus watching everything. Not interrupting, not getting involved, just monitoring. The looks they wore made Mammon feel supported, not chastised. Something he hadn't expected. But Phego had crossed a line, one Bez would probably agree on. Thaus, for all his toughness, had a major soft spot for any Omega, which meant he'd be pissed at Phego's words as well. Phego could bawl the brothers out all he wanted, but never the Omegas. And sure as hell not Charmeine. She was Mammon's mate, and he'd protect her to the end. Over his brothers.

Shit.

Mammon caught Bez's eye, and the man nodded once. Understanding again. Matings changed things, adjusted loyalties and priorities. He hadn't been ready for that. But he would be after tonight.

Phego rubbed his neck and growled low, giving Mammon space but not completely backing down. "Fine. You want her that bad? You need to deal with the fact that her trouble comes with her. Which means you've got us on your ass every minute of every day."

"Fine," Mammon growled. "I'll play by the rules if it means we can get in the game. I want to take these Apex Hunters out, and I'll need you guys to help me." He stalked closer, forcing Phego up against the wall. "But don't talk shit about my mate...ever."

Phego didn't reply at first. He stood and stared at Mammon, weighing his resolve, it seemed. But finally, he nodded. "Fine. My apologies for the earlier comment. It won't happen again."

That apology was more than Mammon could have asked for. "Good. Now, let's plan. I don't want to leave her safety, or that of her friends, to chance."

"That's why we're here. I called in a mated Dire for a reason, too. Fucking mating haze distracting you from the job. It's ridiculous." With that, Phego pushed off the wall and headed back down the hall. Toward where the others still sat, watching, Bez looking almost proud. Yeah, he knew. Mammon had accepted Charmeine as his fated mate tonight. She was *his*, and no one was going to fuck with her ever again

"Take a piss, man," Bez called, finally turning so as not to be staring down the hallway. "Then get back to the table. We've got fucking work to do if we're going to figure out a plan Blaze will accept so we can get rid of these fucking parasites who call themselves Hunters."

Twelve

Charmeine had never been so distracted, especially not from receiving an alert on her phone. But with every text notification, every snippet of words from Mammon, her obsession grew. As did her need for more. She finally understood why humans were always fixated on the handheld devices. Flirting without being in the same room carried a certain sense of freedom. One she enjoyed. And Mammon gave good flirt.

"I've never seen you smile so much."

Charmeine glanced up at Ethan's words. The man stared back, a small, almost sarcastic smile on his face.

"He's funny. Are we almost there yet?"

Ethan glanced out the window. Traffic wasn't moving very quickly. "Five minutes."

"He's going to be mad we're late." Charmeine looked back down as her phone buzzed again. Her mate wanted to meet up with her, to see one another in person again.

Come for a wolf run with me.

Her own inner beast practically whined, desperate to be released…and perhaps rub up against her mate. She'd seen Mammon's wolf already, the amazing Dire Wolf bloodline obvious in every ermine spot and muscled angle, but Charmeine wasn't as ready to let go. The Hunters were skilled at snatching their prey while they were in animal form. It was why she couldn't run as her wolf without security, why she resisted the urge to shift. Why her wolf howled so mournfully every night.

Charmeine typed back a message letting him know she didn't have the time that day. And she didn't. She had a lunch with Finn that they were rushing to, and then she needed to put in what would amount to a full day's work at the rescue. Running with her mate would have to take a backseat.

"We're here," Ethan said. Charmeine peered out the window as the car pulled up outside the restaurant. A pang of longing hit her, one that nearly kept her in her seat. She'd rather be at the O'Rourke estate, Mammon at her side as they argued over books. She'd rather be running through the woods in her wolf form. She'd rather be anywhere but at some fancy restaurant with people watching her every move.

With a deep sigh, she put her phone back in her purse and smoothed her hair. Her need for her mate would have to be put on hold; it was time to go to work.

"There she is." Finn stood with a grin when she walked in, holding out his arms for a hug. Charmeine kissed his cheeks and let him pull her close, giving in to the sudden need she felt for some sort of physical contact. She'd never been particularly affectionate, especially for a wolf shifter. Sure, she and Finn had a certain physical comfort around one another, but even that was restrained and unusual. Most wolves needed touch from their packmates, craved an almost constant connection. But since the death of her parents, she'd avoided such things, had closed herself off into a little box where she could guard her heart. Until she met her mate. Mammon had her all tied up in knots inside, had her wanting things she should have been avoiding, had her needing touch and feel and connection for the first time in her life. Perhaps a day away from him would be a good thing.

"Sorry we're late." Charmeine ripped herself from Finn's embrace, unbalanced by her craving for a different touch. "The conference call with the real estate team ran longer than planned."

"How's that going?" Finn pushed in her chair, then moved to sit across from her, even leaning in as if truly interested in what was happening with the project he saw as solely hers. A fact that made Charmeine smile. This was normal. This she was accustomed to.

"Good. We have solid options down here. It won't be selecting the best of the worst like in other places we discussed."

"That's wonderful news." Finn nodded to the waiter, giving him room to pour wine for the two of them and waiting until the staff had departed to begin again. "I need to apologize about last night. I hadn't planned on leaving you alone with Mammon."

Charmeine fought to keep her heart rate steady. Just hearing his name sent her mind spinning, let alone remembering the feel of him against her, the fire of his tongue on her body.

"It's fine," she said, trying to keep her voice steady. "Mammon was…fine."

Finn's eyebrows jumped, a twitch that told her she hadn't pulled off calm and collected as well as she'd hoped. Thankfully, he didn't mention her tell. He took a sip of water, giving her a moment to collect herself instead. "He seems like a straight-up guy."

Yes, he did. And yet… "How can we ever be sure, though?"

"Instinct, more than anything. Plus, I asked around about him. He's well respected in the local shifter community."

That didn't calm the butterflies, though. "People lie."

"Yes, but he doesn't fit the Hunter type. Especially not with what he told us about his own background."

True, Mammon admitting he was a Dire Wolf seemed like the act of an honest, straightforward man. There could be consequences should that fact get out, ramifications for him and the rest of his pack. He'd trusted her and Finn…or had he played them into thinking he was giving something important away, something that could be used as leverage?

"Money can make anyone a type." Charmeine ran a finger around the edge of her water glass as a heavy cloak of what felt too much like fear blanketed her.

"Is that your phone?" Finn pointed to her purse where something was definitely buzzing. The urge to look, to check for messages, was strong. But not strong enough.

"I'm sure it's nothing." She pasted on her best smile and picked up her menu, ignoring another buzz from her bag. "Should we order soon? I've been craving something sweet since I woke up."

———

"And you got the extra blankets?" Charmeine checked over her list one last time.

Ethan stretched and cracked his neck. "Blankets, bottles, six types of pacifiers, pink slippers with glittery decorations, and a princess nightgown. All purchased, unpacked, and in place."

He made her life so much easier. "Thank you. With four intakes and the surprise of little Emerson—"

"Stop," Ethan chuckled and shook his head. "It was a busy day, and having a small child show up with a family we had recorded as only made up of two adults threw a wrench in our plans. But we did it…everyone is in, safe, and comfortable for the night."

Charmeine grinned. As tired as she was, there was still a sense of pride within her. A happiness that grew from knowing she'd done her job well. "Another day down."

"Another day down." Ethan yawned and nodded toward the front entrance. "Are you heading back to the house?"

"No. I want to get a few more things done before I call it a night. But you should go."

Ethan paused, obviously torn between his need for sleep and whatever loyalty had kept him by her side for so many years. "Are you sure? I can wait for you."

"No. Go back to Finn's. I'm just going to catch up on some paperwork."

Ethan nodded once. "If you say so, boss. Don't work too late."

"Have a good night." Charmeine watched him walk away before heading for her office at the front of the building. She'd needed a place to work without being distracted, so she'd chosen an exam room off an unused hallway. It wasn't ideal, but it was private enough for her to be able to concentrate, which was all she could really hope for.

The sun had long ago set, the families mostly bedded down for the night. It had been a good day. One she hoped she could call an end to within the next few hours.

Her phone buzzed right as she turned toward the wing where the new families had been placed. She pulled it from her pocket, her heart heavy, her stomach suddenly in knots. Another text from Mammon. Another one ignored. She'd been so busy, so backlogged, that she just hadn't taken the time to keep up the conversation. At least, that's what she told herself.

But still, her heart leaped every time she read his flirty words.

Twenty-four hours ago, we were discussing Judy Bloom. And then…

Charmeine sighed. *And then,* all right. And then she'd lost herself to the heavy, aching need within her to claim that man. To the primal desires that fogged her mind and ran rampant all over her heart.

Not tonight.

Don't you work? How can you possibly spend your entire day texting me when you should be doing something productive?

This IS productive. Talking to you is the most productive thing I've ever done.

Oooh, that was a good one. Charmeine nearly bought that line. *You can't charm me.*

I can try.

She bit her lip, thinking over what to reply, but a sudden scream broke the silence of the night and sent her heart racing for an entirely different reason. Without thought, she ran down the hall, growling with every step. Not here, not tonight. Not on her watch. The Hunters had better not be trying to attack, or she'd lose her mind. They weren't ready for a full assault.

But there was no attack, no bad guys to vanquish or threat to handle. There was just a little girl in a pink nightgown clinging to a stuffed wolf…and crying.

"Emerson?" Charmeine slid to her knees, grabbing ahold of the shaking child and pulling her into a hug. "What's wrong, baby? Why are you screaming?"

"I thought they were back."

"Who?" But she knew. She always knew. Every child, every adult, every shifter affected by the Apex Hunters had the same bad dreams. She knew their nightmares.

She'd lived them.

Emerson cuddled closer, gasping through her tears. "The bad guys who killed my parents. I kept seeing them. I thought they were here."

Charmeine shushed the little girl, rocking her in her arms. "No, baby. Not here. They're definitely not here."

"How do you know?"

And wasn't that the worst possible question? "I don't. Not for sure. But I have faith. We're guarded here. I don't think they can get in."

The little girl nodded but still held on, which suited Charmeine fine. She rocked and shushed and hummed, calming both of them down. Other shifters peeked out into the hall but left the two alone, all of them understanding the situation. All of them having had the same bad dreams, probably. Watching their families die over and over behind their eyes, waking up screaming or having soiled their bed. The fear and the disgust throwing them into a state of panic so strong, there was no way around it. Yeah. They all knew.

When Emerson finally sagged in her arms, sleepy and ready to go back to bed, Charmeine scooped her up and rose to her feet. The poor baby weighed almost nothing, the couple she'd come in with having no idea how long she'd been alone before they found her. A single survivor of an attack on a tiny little nothing of a pack—just as Charmeine had been.

She carried the girl to her bed, making sure to tuck her and her stuffed wolf in nice and tight. Her mind spiraling around memories of Finn's mom doing the same thing for her. Of her own mom...

"Miss Charmeine?"

Two big, brown eyes stared up at her, tears ready to fall, making Charmeine's heart hurt to the point of breaking. "Yes, Emerson?"

"Why did they do this to us?"

Fighting back tears of her own, Charmeine ran her fingers over Emerson's cheek. The little girl's scars were almost hidden in the dark, but Charmeine had seen them enough to picture them clearly. Deep, dark tracks all the way from her scalp to her throat. Claw marks. Ones that had never healed and never would, that would forever remind the girl of all she'd been through. All she'd lost. But Charmeine knew those jagged tracks were nothing compared to the scars inside.

"They're bad people, Emerson. There's no rhyme or reason to why…just hate and anger brewing within them to the point of evil."

"How do we stop them?"

"We love." Charmeine's heart jumped, her thoughts flittering toward Mammon. "The only cure for hate is love. Don't let them make you hate or turn you bitter or angry. Don't let them win."

"I'll try, but they scare me." The little girl yawned and cuddled her wolf closer.

Charmeine kissed the girl's forehead and stood to leave, her thoughts focused on one thing. *They scare me, too.*

Words she could never admit. Not to the refugees she supported, and certainly not to anyone she knew. Well, maybe…

Once back in the hall, Charmeine pulled her phone from her pocket. She didn't even look at the texts waiting for her, assuming they were all from Mammon. She was too tired, physically and mentally, to flirt or tease. She needed more than words on a screen. Craved something deeper. She stepped into a closet meant to hold janitorial supplies, one they hadn't filled yet, and she pressed a button on her phone.

And then she waited.

"Hello?" Mammon's surprised voice was a balm to her

weary soul, something she hadn't truly realized she needed until it wrapped around her.

"Hi. It's me…Charmeine."

He chuckled softly. "I know, baby."

The endearment caused a fire to simmer low in her gut. A good one. "You sounded surprised."

"I was more taken aback that this damn phone rang. I didn't know people still used them to actually speak."

Charmeine huffed a soft laugh, letting the stress roll off her shoulders with every second. "Yeah, there *is* a lot of texting and emailing in the world."

He hummed, a deep throaty sound that had her dying to crawl through the phone and curl up with him. To be in the dark with him, alone and safe. To allow him to protect her, even if for just a moment.

"I like texting. So long as it's with you," Mammon said, his voice deep and smooth. "But I like this whole speaking thing much more. Though not as much as being in the same room with you. That'd have to be my favorite."

Hers too, not that she was ready to tell him that. Still, there were things she needed to say. Words she owed him.

"I'm sorry," she whispered, hoping she sounded as sincere as the words felt to her.

"For what?"

"For what I said the other night. How I…dismissed you."

"You don't need to apologize, Char. Not for protecting yourself. Not ever. Besides, cuddling's totally overrated. I'd take a blow job any day over that."

Charmeine laughed, the sound slightly sad and weak, running her fingers along dusty shelves as she paced. If only she knew, if she could be sure.

"What's on your mind, beautiful?"

But surety was not something she could find in an empty

janitor's closet. "Nothing."

"Liar." He spoke the word on a growl, but that wasn't what brought on a shiver.

"What if you're the liar?" She froze as the line went silent, as she waited for something from him. An answer of some sort. What she needed, she didn't know. What she wanted, well…she wanted truth and confidence. Things she didn't know how to get.

Finally, Mammon sighed. "You know I work for the president of the NALB?"

Charmeine frowned, not sure where that subject change came from. "Yes."

"The man has a mate named Dante. Well, he has two now, but the third wasn't in the picture a few years ago and so isn't important to this story."

"Okay."

"The president has a staff, as you can imagine. Everything from cooks to people who clean the mansion to fifteen levels of guards. All vetted, all investigated and approved to work in direct contact with our leaders."

None of that surprised Charmeine.

"One day while I was at Merriweather Fields, I happened to overhear a conversation between a couple of those guards. There was nothing overt about it—no threat or whispered plans for treasonous acts. A simple conversation, but something about it struck me as wrong, so I started a quiet investigation into them and their teams. An enemy of the president had gotten to them from the outside, paid them off to supply information on the mate's schedule and guard staff. These so-called guards were selling out their employers, the men they'd taken a vow to protect, and that level of greed infuriated me."

"What happened?" Charmeine held her breath, practically shaking with the need to know what came next.

Mammon stayed quiet for a long moment, but when he did answer, his voice was darker. Lower. Rough and dangerous. "I killed every guard involved."

Oh God, that snarl should not be sexy considering the subject. But it was. It *so* was. She swallowed hard. "Deservedly so, it seems."

"Yes, deservedly so. But what I did next tends to be the act the rest of the staff remembers most."

"What did you do?"

"See, the traitors had gotten access to critical information simply by being stationed outside the president's private wing. They could hear conversations going on inside his suite through the main doors. I built a frame in the hallway to add another set of doors beyond the main ones, these thicker and more solid. Soundproofing the residence."

"Why would that be something to talk about?"

"Because I didn't just build a frame and a slab of wood for the doors. I carved images into them. I set up a little workstation right out front of the main entrance to the mansion, and I spent weeks carving woodland scenes and polishing the slabs until they were truly works of art, if I can be so bold as to call my own scratching art."

Charmeine smiled at his humble words. She didn't believe him, but she still smiled. "Modesty suits you, but I'm still not understanding—"

"I carved them with the claws and teeth of the traitors I killed on behalf of the president."

Charmeine released a breath, surprising herself with the soft rushing sound. "That sounds…horrible."

"No, baby. It wasn't. It was a teaching moment for the rest of the staff. Those bastards had focused on the one they saw as the weakest link in an effort to overthrow the president. They used their job, their position of trust, for profit. I won't tolerate deception from within."

She clenched her hand into a fist and closed her eyes. He seemed like such a good man, an honest one. A loyal one. But still, she wasn't sure…she didn't know what she needed to *be* sure, but she didn't have it. Not yet.

Mammon must have taken her silence for what it was because when he spoke again, his voice was softer. More cajoling. Enticing. "I would never manipulate you like that. I would never let anyone hurt you from within the walls you build around you. I swear it."

Hot, angry tears fell faster than she could wipe them away. "I don't know how to trust you."

Mammon must have sighed, the sound creating static in her ear. "Keep talking, baby. That's how we build trust. We just keep talking."

Charmeine nodded, not yet ready to fully agree. To let him know she might be willing to try something new. But she slid to the floor, her back against a stone wall, and she did what he suggested.

"So… How was your day?"

Mammon hummed again. "Why don't you tell me about yours instead?"

She sighed again, her body and mind sagging in exhaustion. "It's been a long day."

"I've got nothing but time, Char. Tell me all about it."

She looked up at the ceiling, letting his voice blanket her in warmth, in comfort, in something that felt alarmingly like…hope.

Charmeine took a deep breath, leaned against the wall, and let go.

"A new mated pair arrived today, and they brought an orphaned little girl in with them. Her family was attacked and burned out of their home by the Hunters. She can't be more than four, and she has this adorable stuffed wolf that she carries everywhere …"

Thirteen

The phone ringing yanked Mammon from a sleep that had been filled with thoughts of his mate. He would have destroyed the infernal device, but the possibility that Charmeine could be on the other end kept him from throwing it across the room. Still, he wanted to. Badly.

Fuck, it was early.

"Hello?" His mumbled greeting sounded horrible, even to his own ears.

The voice from the other end was far smoother. "President Blasius Zenne requests your presence this morning."

That woke him up. "Dante?"

"Who else would it be, Dire Mammon? Are you agreeable to meeting your president?"

"When and where?"

"Sycamore Strip. We land at ten. I recommend you be on time."

The call disconnected, leaving Mammon holding the silent phone in his hand for a long, painful minute. When the screen went dark, he pressed the button again. The date stared him in the face, a taunting presence he'd almost been able to disregard. Luc had given him two weeks, and that deadline had passed without his noticing. He was so utterly screwed. Pursuing the O'Rourke pack had gone completely against orders, but that hadn't stopped him. And though he had the fact that his mate was associated with that pack, he doubted Blasius would let him off the hook. There were rules and regulations, procedures, and a chain of command. Mammon had said fuck you to all of them.

And he'd do it again…for Charmeine.

Mammon shot a quick text to Deus to let the shifter know why he'd be on the move so early—because the nosy fucker would totally notice such a thing—then jumped out of bed. He needed a shower, a quick jack-off to lose the hard-on dreaming of his mate had left him with, and coffee…not necessarily in that order.

Twenty minutes, one shower wank, and two cups of coffee later, Mammon rolled out of the parking lot, revved the engine of his motorcycle for a little extra fuck you to the world, and roared toward the highway. Time was on his side, and traffic was light. He could make it to the airstrip before the presidential plane touched down. His motorcycle was definitely up to the challenge, speeding past the few cars on the road with ease. The throaty rumble comforted him, soothing his frazzled nerves a bit. Blasius wouldn't kill him; he wouldn't kick him out of the Dire Wolves, either. They were a pack, a family based on more than orders and rank. Blasius had no control over that and little control over them, to be honest. Luc set the rules, and currently his rule was they worked for the NALB president on missions as assigned. They hadn't always, though…and wouldn't forever.

But what Blasius *could* do was tell Mammon he couldn't be involved in NALB missions, which would put stress on his pack. They usually worked alone or in teams of two to three, but sometimes, jobs were too big and risks were too high for a small team. On those jobs, they all showed up. With only seven of them, each Dire had to pull his weight in a group mission. And they'd always been a team of seven. With only six, training would need to be reworked, and the guys would be in danger until they figured out the new dynamic. A thought that had Mammon growling into the wind.

Halfway to the airport, though, Mammon spotted a tail. A big SUV followed him—a Suburban—the tinted windows not giving away the driver. Soon after, the Suburban was joined by a Jeep. Still dark. Totally dangerous. Both more calming than not.

He knew those vehicles.

When a third vehicle he recognized joined the other two, Mammon laughed. His pack wasn't going to let him down or send him to fight alone. He hadn't asked for backup, hadn't requested a show of solidarity, but Deus must have called one in. His brothers, his team, his pack…they wouldn't leave a man to fight alone, no matter how badly he'd screwed up.

Mammon pulled up outside the hangar five minutes early for his meeting and parked his bike to the side. His brothers followed suit, lining up their cars at an angle to make a quick escape easier. Old habits died hard. The three Dires converged with Mammon in front of the hangar door. Phego, Thaus, and Bez, looking ready for a battle Mammon was hoping he wouldn't have to fight.

"You didn't need to come," Mammon said, eyeing each man individually.

Bez grunted. "No Dire fights alone if he doesn't have to."

Mammon nodded, knowing he was right. "Think he's here to say hi?"

"I think he's here to kick your ass for your O'Rourke obsession."

Phego scowled. "We should have notified the NALB earlier."

Thaus, looking tired and weaker than Mammon would have liked, let out a deep breath. "Without a solid plan, he would have forced Mammon and his mate to separate until the threat passed. She's an Omega, which makes her the priority to Blasius."

Even the thought made a fiery rage blanket Mammon. No. Not happening. His mate was staying where he could help protect her, period. But before Mammon could respond, a small plane taxied over from one of the runways. The four men formed a triangle of sorts—Mammon at the front, the rest backing him up. Ready and waiting to greet their President.

They didn't have to wait long. A guard unknown to Mammon opened the door of the plane and lowered the stairs to the ground. Dante and Blasius stepped out, both men pausing and frowning when they saw who all was waiting for them.

Surprise.

"I seem to remember a scene very much like this not too long ago, Beelzebub," Blasius said as he stepped onto the tarmac.

"And you'll see it again and again, President Blasius. We're pack, and we stand together."

Blasius looked over each man in turn, seemingly sizing them up. "Not all your men stand together, it seems."

Bez growled, low and long. A challenge of sorts toward the most powerful shifter on the continent. Mammon wasn't sure if he was suicidal or just stupid, but the growling indicated one of the two for sure.

Phego jumped in, perhaps trying to cover the growl

of the other Dire. "Luc is running a mission out of Alaska. Levi and Deus are up east setting up security for Levi's new mate. I assume you remember how territorial and defensive a newly mated wolf is, sir, and that you can understand the need for Deus to stay by Levi's side until the younger Dire settles into his new role."

President Blasius frowned. "Yes. Of course."

Mammon almost relaxed, almost took a deep breath, but then Blasius turned his glare on him, and his wolf rushed forth, ready to defend them. Ready to fight anyone who tried to get between him and his mate.

"You disobeyed a direct order."

Mammon could only nod. "I did, sir."

"I told you to leave the O'Rourke pack alone."

"Yes, you did."

"Then explain yourself, soldier."

Something about his tone, about the demand from a wolf who technically wasn't his Alpha, set Mammon's teeth on edge and made his wolf push forward even more. If his eyes weren't already silver with the coming beast, they soon would be. It was that anger, the pride of the Dire in him, that pushed Mammon past the point of fear or anxiousness and over to the other side. The darker side. The angry one.

"Did you know the Apex Hunters are still around?" Mammon asked, a definite rumble under his words.

Blasius cocked his head, looking curious. "That was a long time ago, Dire Mammon, but I remember ordering their decimation."

"Not decimated, sir. There're a handful still out there. They've rebanded, and they're killing shifter families again. They're after the pack I monitor."

Dante stepped forward on that one. "Proof?"

"Just the word of the O'Rourkes." *And Charmeine Byrne,* he finished in his thoughts, though he didn't say the words.

Dante scoffed. "No confirmation. And that rumor definitely isn't a good enough reason for you to break rank the way you did."

Mammon growled again, his hands curling into fists. If he could just get his point across. "Sir, if you'd listen to the—"

But Blasius had apparently had enough. "I want you back in Chicago today for a disciplinary hearing."

The world went silent except for the howling of Mammon's wolf in his head. Long, soulful howls of pain and anger. His mate was in danger, and he was being taken from her side. No fucking way. He couldn't leave Charmeine unprotected. Wouldn't. Ever.

Mammon said the one thing he possibly could in that moment.

"No."

The word was a bitter bite, a sign of disobeying he wasn't necessarily proud of, but there was no other way. His mate had become more important than the man the Dires *allowed* to lead them. Her safety and comfort were his primary concern, and she would not be safe without Mammon close by. She needed him, and he needed her. Story done.

Blasius dropped the shock off his face and snarled, taking two threatening steps forward. "Pardon me?"

But Mammon wasn't backing down. Not completely. Not on this. "With all due respect, sir, I said no."

"Do you want to explain to me—"

"Finn O'Rourke was raised with a little girl whose family was killed by the Apex Hunters. Omega shewolf Charmeine Byrne, heir to the Byrne fortune. She's staying with Finn now as they build a safe place for the refugees left behind by these sick bastards. She is vital to their safety." Mammon took a deep breath, letting his growl rumble through him loud and clear. Making his point known. "And she's my mate. Charmeine Byrne is mine, and I won't leave her unprotected."

Blasius and Dante stood silent and staring, probably a bit shocked. Mammon could understand that. After centuries of no mates, three Dires had managed to locate the women the fates deemed as their perfect matches within the last twelve months.

But Blasius' shock didn't negate the fact Mammon had a mate to protect. A woman with an important job protecting others. He would stay by her side until the threat was completely eliminated, until every Apex Hunter was tracked down and slaughtered for their role in trying to destroy the shifter community. Mammon wouldn't leave Charmeine's side… Whether she wanted him there or not.

And he needed to make *that* point clear.

Mammon lifted his chin, looking his president directly in the eye. "I won't leave her."

Blasius stared past the Dires, his eyes seeking something that wasn't there. "The Dire Wolves have walked the earth longer than any known creature. I'm not even sure there are vampires as old as you seven. In all that time, not a one found their mate. And yet, we've had three in a year. All to Omega females."

Bez growled softly behind Mammon, probably feeling some sort of protectiveness toward Sariel. He was the first Dire to be gifted a mate by the fates. The Dire had struggled with finding the balance between mission and mate at that time, but he'd come out okay. He'd managed to save the women he was after and complete the mission. Technically, Mammon didn't have a sanctioned mission to end the Apex Hunters, but he didn't care. It was his turn, and he would not let his mate down. Fuck procedure.

Growls grew louder, rumbling closer to snarls. The Dires all stood on edge, ready to fight, ready to defend what they saw as an attack on one of their own. Mammon could feel it in the air, sense it. No one threatened a Dire Wolf, and the mates were Dires in their eyes.

"Stand down, Beelzebub," Dante called, keeping his voice low but firm. Ordering. Phego and Thaus responded with their own growls of warning, adding to the tension of the moment. This crew was a powder keg ready to blow, but Mammon didn't have time for that.

"Sir," Mammon called, taking another step forward. "I fucked up by breaking rank and disobeying orders. I'll come to Chicago for a hearing on that once I know my mate is safe. But right now, I'm not leaving her. The Hunters are out there, and they're hunting the only Byrne left—my Charmeine. She rescues others in her place, creates a safe place for them, and joins them together into a pack. That's part of her Omega power, I believe—bringing the unlikely survivors together to form a unit. I need to be here to help protect them all. There are children, sir. I won't leave them to be slaughtered in their sleep."

Blasius refocused on the Dires, his head cocked, the anger gone. "We need more proof of the Apex Hunters before we accept that they're back."

"Then we'll get it," Bez said with a snarl.

Mammon nodded. "We will. This group, they pay off the people close to their victims, manipulate extended family, and seek to destroy their victims from the inside. They target the weakest links, like the children. They are the epitome of evil, and it's time to take them down. Dire style."

Dante very nearly smirked. "And what exactly is Dire style?"

This time, Thaus answered. "Completely wipe them out. To do the job right the first time and not leave it for someone else to clean up later."

"Exactly." Mammon nodded, trying not to amplify the

shot Thaus just fired at their bosses. The ones who'd ordered the destruction of the Apex Hunters' pack…and failed to see it through. "The O'Rourkes can't take them out alone, and the refugees aren't soldiers or fighters in any respect. They need all of us."

"And as always, the Dire Wolves are standing behind one of their own," Bez said. "Mammon and Charmeine are mated, which makes her pack. We *will* protect our pack at all costs."

Blasius sighed, looking to Dante as if for reason. His dark-skinned mate simply stared back. Silent. Giving the president the responsibility of the decision.

"Fine," Blasius said, biting out his word before heading for the plane. "Call in anyone you need to help keep the Omega safe, and get me proof of the Hunters. But whether you find it or not, we will deal with this insubordination, Dire Mammon."

"Understood." Mammon nodded and took a few steps back. Joining his brothers shoulder to shoulder instead of in an attack formation. As soon as Dante and Blasius were back on board their small private plane, the Dires huddled closer. Went to work.

Phego started, looking from one man to the next. "How do we destroy the Hunters?"

"Same thing we always do," Bez said. "Research, plan, track, and destroy."

Mammon could only grin. "Ooh Rah."

Fourteen

"There isn't enough." Charmeine sighed and looked over the printouts again. "How can there not be enough? I thought we had the money from Finn set aside for additional expenses."

Ethan typed something into his computer, not meeting her eyes. "Expenses are higher because of the number of refugees needing long-term housing and care. Plus, we weren't expecting so many young children."

Charmeine bit back another sigh that really wanted to come out as a growl. He was right, but that didn't make the news any easier to take. Something wasn't sitting well with the books. Finn had been very generous with her, giving her everything she asked for and more so she could continue trying to help the families almost destroyed by the Apex Hunters. The families like her own. Still, the generosity wasn't assumed or accepted without a heavy responsibility. She worked tirelessly to make every dollar stretch, every cent give meaning and be useful. She didn't like knowing the account she managed had a balance far lower than expected and not to be able to figure out why.

She was going to have to do something she hated doing. "I'll ask Finn for more money until my accounts are transferred over."

"Fine. What about—"

Charmeine snatched her phone off the table as it pinged. She'd become addicted to that noise. Mammon had been sending little notes, small messages that let her know he was thinking about her. And she loved them. Plus, they were a simple way to get to know him better. Every word sent was another building block on the path to friendship…and maybe more.

But building that path would be a slow journey, and communicating solely via text message wouldn't speed up the process. Still, she liked hearing from him and missed him when he wasn't available for their back-and-forth. It didn't help that she hadn't seen him in almost a week. True, that was mostly her fault—her busy schedule with the rescue keeping her tied up most days—but she missed the big lug. She wanted to see his face, to smell his earthy scent, to remember the touch of his finger against her cheek. She wanted, and knowing that desire was the mating haze didn't lessen the draw. She wanted, and he wasn't available in anything other than electronic form at the moment.

When she opened the message, a giggle slipped out. He'd sent her a picture of a wolf winking, with the phrase *Howl you doin'?* in big letters across the top. It was cute, funny, and perfectly him…from what she knew.

"Again with this?"

Ethan's obvious disgust flipped Charmeine's emotions from happy to irritated in a simple three words. She shrugged, setting her phone back on the table, facedown.

"He's funny," she said, returning her attention to the

spreadsheets he'd printed for her. But Ethan wasn't through… and he knew enough about Charmeine to hit where it hurt.

"Will he still be funny when he slaughters the children?"

Charmeine's growl was vicious, her wolf taking more control than she'd let the beast have in months. "He would never do that."

But even as she spoke the words, that rock of guilt landed in her gut. How *could* she know that? What if? What if the Hunters had gotten to him? What if the whole Dire Wolf admission was a lie? What if he was a lot more dangerous and deceptive than she assumed? It could happen, and the lives at stake weren't hers to risk.

And yet…

"I need an iced tea." Ethan set his laptop aside and stood, looking frustrated and angry. "Can I get you anything?"

Charmeine shook her head, still stuck in her thoughts. Thoughts of the big man with the big secret who promised her things she wasn't sure he would deliver on. How could she know if she could trust him? What was trust, anyway? And how could she risk so many innocent lives on the chance that he truly was trustworthy?

Feeling as if she'd lost some sort of tether tying her to her life, Charmeine did the only thing she could think of to find solid footing. She grabbed her phone and sent a text.

Where are you?

Home. Are you okay?

She bit her lip. Was she? Okay seemed so far away, and the tornado inside of her was spinning so out of control. She could only answer honestly.

I don't know.

His response was immediate. *Where are you? Do you need me?*

Charmeine closed her eyes, that fear, the distrust, burning hot and bright.

I'm at the rescue.

Can I come to you? Let me help you.

Her fear flared, the tug between the two sides of herself growing stronger. To trust him or not to trust him. To let him in or keep him out. To...

A picture of a smiling Emerson flashed across her mind, making her decision an easy one. Her fingers didn't even shake as she typed.

No.

When Mammon responded, it wasn't with comforting words or questions. No angry reply about her distrust or promises. It was with an address. A simple street number and name, and it was the most perfect answer ever.

Ethan walked back into the room, iced tea in hand, as Charmeine tucked her phone in her purse.

"Change of plans," Charmeine said, heading for the door.

He froze, staring at her, his mouth agape. "We're not through. Where are you going?"

Good question, but one she wasn't quite ready to answer. "Out."

"Out where? And with whom?" Ethan's questions sounded like accusations, something Charmeine refused to acknowledge.

"It's none of your business, Ethan."

"But there's work to be done."

Charmeine's heels clacked against the tiled floors, quick and bright to her ears. The sound of freedom moving closer. Of a temporary escape. "I'll be back to handle the finances in a few hours."

"You can't just walk out. There are...things. You're needed here." Ethan chased after her.

"I'm not walking out, I'm taking a break." Or that's what she told herself. Truthfully, she wasn't sure what she was doing. But she liked it, liked the way it felt right to be heading toward someone instead of away from them. And she wasn't stopping.

"So this low-class guy is worth more than your family? More than the children you claim to want to save?"

Ethan's words brought Charmeine to a physical stop. Her wolf growled again, the sound reverberating through her chest. Echoing off the bare walls. Reminding her of her inner strength, the part of herself she kept under lock and key. A warning to anyone trying to get in her way. Her turn to face her arrogant cousin was a slow one, a precise one. The turn of an animal ready to strike back at an attacker.

"Listen to me, Ethan, and listen well. I won't repeat myself." She stalked closer, threatening with her posture and her stare, keeping her growl loud and strong. "This has been my entire world for years; it is my focus and my priority. But I have found my mate, and my world needs to adjust to accommodate him. So this *low-class* guy? He's going to be sticking around and possibly taking up some of my time. If you can't handle that, you know damn well where the door is."

And with that, she turned and strode for that same door, ready for something more than accounting logs and criticism. Ready for her mate to soothe her heart if only for a few moments.

Fifteen

W hat else?" Mammon paced, wanting to crawl through the phone and kick Deus in the shin. The man had the worst possible timing.

"I need to run a few more cables at the diner, but otherwise, the job is done. Amy wasn't a fan of wearing the tracker device like the one I sent you, but I think Levi can convince her."

Mammon snorted. "Because Levi will drive her nuts until she does."

"True that. It would have been easier to use her phone like standard Dire procedure, but apparently she takes it out of her pocket when working. She likes to be *unplugged* in the kitchen."

The shock and disgust in Deus' voice wasn't a surprise. The man probably never unplugged, his entire life lived in pixels and code. He rarely even interacted with his Dire brothers much anymore except over the phone or the computer; he certainly wouldn't understand choosing to interact in the human world. Relating to a woman who spent her days feeding people was something the shifter probably couldn't do. Like, ever.

The door to the apartment opened, and Mammon nearly jumped across the room. Phego walked in, meeting his anxious gaze with a furrow of his brow. Shit, he needed to settle down. He'd sent her the text with his address on a whim, not knowing exactly what she'd do with it. Not really planning anything…but then the reality hit that she could show up at his apartment. And he wanted that; he wanted that so badly, he could hardly sit still as he waited.

But so far, Charmeine hadn't shown up. He'd sent her his address not knowing what she would do, and apparently, that answer was nothing. No response, no driving over. So Mammon paced, and he fought back the urge to ask Deus if he'd zeroed in on her cell phone signal enough to know where she was. That would be a breach of trust—she wasn't ready to tell him where the rescue facility was, and he refused to push that point. So with no intel, he waited for her to make a move and got irritated with his brothers for taking up the time he should have been using to obsess over where his mate was and what she was thinking.

When exactly he drifted back to his puberty years, he wasn't sure, but that's sure as shit what it felt like.

"That Phego?" Deus asked, probably seeing the blip from the other Dire's tracking device in his phone. Which was sort of creepy, though Mammon knew the Dire monitored them to help keep them safe. Or at least, he hoped that was all. Deus always did have some voyeuristic tendencies, even long before the digital age came upon them.

"Yeah." Mammon gave Phego a chin nod. He stopped pacing, turning all his attention to his brother, noting the stiff set to his shoulders and the frown on his face. Phego wasn't exactly Mr. Personality, but this was much more harsh than usual. "What's happening?"

"We've run into a problem."

It was Deus who answered. "What sort of problem?"

"Tracking pings."

Deus cursed, which told Mammon the bad news was bad. He just didn't know how bad.

"What does that mean?" Mammon asked, looking from Phego to the phone and back. He didn't care who gave him the answer so long as someone explained.

It was Deus who responded. "It means someone knows we're searching for them."

Okay, that was pretty bad. "Shit."

A knock on the door broke the moment, dropping tension on the guys like a dump truck. Mammon froze, ready to fight off whoever was on the other side if needed, suddenly expecting the Hunters to barge in or something. Luckily, Phego kept his head. He gave the signal for silence and crept to the door. Mammon waited, tense and ready for just about anything…except what was on the other side.

Mate.

The second Phego pulled the door open the first inch, Mammon was in motion.

"Oh. Uh…is Mammon—" Before Charmeine could finish her question to Phego, Mammon was there. Pushing his Dire brother to the side and pulling her into his room. His wolf chuffed in his mind. Safe…she was safe and with him in his den. Their den. Safe.

Mammon nuzzled into her neck for one moment, then pulled away, happy that his scent was on her even if it wasn't strong yet. He'd fix that later.

"What are you doing here?" he asked, unable to stop the stupid question from falling from his lips.

Her face blanched, an embarrassed sort of flush rising along her neck. A flush that made Mammon feel about three feet tall. What the hell was he thinking?

"Hang on," he said when she tried to pull away. "Let me try that again with a little more thought." He ran his hands over her arms, sighing, letting his relief show. "It's so good to see you."

She hesitated for a moment, watching him warily, but then she gave in. She curled into his chest, her arms going around his waist. Mammon clung to her, growling softly as he felt her sag and relax into his hold. Oblivious to anything but her.

"I'm sorry I just came over like this," she said, making Mammon chuckle.

"Never be sorry for coming to see me. Not ever. I'm glad you're here." He pulled back, regaining himself and suddenly aware of both how hard he was with her pressed against him and the fact that he had one brother on the phone and another in the room. Something Charmeine definitely paid attention to as she eyed Phego over Mammon's shoulder. Shit.

"Am I interrupting something?" she asked, glancing from Phego to Mammon and back.

"Not at all." Mammon subtly adjusted himself before pulling her to his side and turning to face Phego. "This is my Dire pack brother, Phego. Phego, this is Charmeine. My mate."

Phego glanced at Mammon before taking a step closer. "It's nice to meet you, Omega Charmeine."

"Nice…to meet you as well." She didn't reach for his hand, didn't offer her arm in greeting as shifters tended to do. In fact, she retreated a bit, nudging her way deeper into Mammon's side. Away from Phego. The two stood in silence, watching each other. Waiting for…something.

Something Deus provided.

"I'm going to hang up now."

Charmeine jumped, but Mammon held her tight. Soothing her, he hoped. "Got it. Let me know when you're finished there. And Phego will call you from his place with the details of the pings."

"Understood," Deus said. "I'm assuming I'm coming to Texas after this? Same stats as with Levi?"

Mammon couldn't look at Charmeine. There was no way she was ready for the amount of protective measures he'd eventually demand for her. Hell, he was stunned she'd even dared to come to his apartment. She wasn't exactly the leap before looking type, and she probably wouldn't like the idea of some stranger tracking her every move from a random computer across the country. No, his mate wasn't going to be as easy to convince as Levi's Amy. Not at all.

Still…

"Yeah. Join us down here when you're done." Mammon grabbed the phone and swiped to end the call. One brother down, one to go.

"I'm out as well." Phego seemed to be reading Mammon's mind. He nodded to Charmeine as a way to say good-bye, but as he walked past, he nudged Mammon in the shoulder. "And I thought Levi mated up."

Mammon's soft growl was unintentional, but deserved. His mate was gorgeous, he knew this. But hearing it from another man—even his brother—set his wolf on edge. Not that Phego cared. He walked out the door chuckling, probably calculating how long it would take Mammon to settle into being mated. Answer? A long fucking time, but the Dire would enjoy every damn second.

As soon as Phego closed the door, Charmeine sagged in what appeared to be relief. "Who's Levi? The man on the phone?"

"No." Mammon stepped back and took her in, noticing the way she curled in on herself, the fear in her stance.

Noticing it and hating it. "Levi is another brother of mine, but he wasn't on the phone."

"How many brothers do you have?" She tracked him, refusing to let him get behind her. A smart and tactical move. A very telling one as well.

Mammon stopped, inching closer. Making sure he didn't spook her. "There are seven of us left."

Charmeine nodded. "And…children?"

"None. But only two brothers have found their mates, outside of me."

"Outside of you," she whispered in return. "Family bonds are so important."

"They are," Mammon replied, skimming her arm with his fingers. "As are mating ones."

Charmeine grew tense again, but her growl told him how much she liked his words. Liked the thought of being tied to him. Even if she wasn't ready to admit it fully.

"What are you doing here?" he whispered, his voice heavy and dark with all the emotions flying through him.

Charmeine shrugged, a move that didn't fit the persona she wore. An action that screamed how far from normal she felt. "I needed to see you."

"I'm here."

Huge blue eyes met his own wide eyes. Filled with a little bit of fear and a hell of a lot of lust. "I know."

"Now what?" Mammon wouldn't push her, wouldn't influence her either. She'd come this far; she was going to have to cross that finish line. Needed to trust *herself* enough to ask for what she wanted.

Her hands gripped his biceps, pulling him closer and holding him back all at once. "I… I don't know."

He leaned down and nuzzled her neck, scenting along the muscles there again. Practically purring as he teased her.

"What do you want, Char?" he whispered when he made

it to her ear. He placed a kiss there, barely brushing her skin with his. She jerked and sighed, her nails almost sinking into his flesh as she gripped his arms tighter. Pulled him closer. As she surrendered fully.

"You." Her answer was quiet and breathy—a true sign of desire.

Mammon surrendered, too. "So have me."

Charmeine couldn't breathe. She could barely stay on her feet. Every inch of her ached for her mate to come closer, every heartbeat called his name. There was nothing but her and him and the mating haze wrapping around them. The one she'd been avoiding. The one she suddenly wanted to surrender to.

"Mammon." She tried to tell him she couldn't, that she needed and wanted but didn't know what to do. That she had no idea how to handle the myriad feelings racing through her. That she wasn't prepared for what this would all mean. All she could say, though, was his name. A single, desperate word…a two-syllable plea. One he must have understood.

Mammon grabbed her, lifting her right off the floor and pulling her tight against him. *Finally.* She sagged in his hold, releasing every ounce of control she'd curated for so many years. Giving herself over to the desire, her body buzzing as it met his.

She would never get enough of that feeling. "Thank you."

His growl was immediate, his hand dropping to grip her ass in a strong, claiming sort of grasp. "Don't thank me yet, baby. I'm getting as much out of this as you are."

He pressed his hips into her, letting her feel him, pushing that hard cock against where she was so hot and swollen for him. And she liked it. She liked it a lot. Already, her mouth watered, remembering the taste of him. The feel of his skin against her tongue. The way his body bowed and his muscles clenched as he came. She shivered, moaning as she recalled how he teased her, how he pressed and pulled and sucked. How he made her come on his tongue.

"Damn it, Char." Mammon carried her across the room, his steps quick. She shouldn't have liked being carried that way, shouldn't have surrendered to the manhandling, but she did. Liked seeing how strong he was, how confident and sure. How in command. She could surrender to him, could give up running and, just for a little while, let him lead her. And she would.

Mammon laid her on the bed, crawling over her, once again pressing the length of his cock against her. "Tell me no."

She grabbed his shoulders, arms languid and slow, voice thick as she asked, "Why?"

Mammon shook his head, rolling his hips into hers and looking so very tortured. "I can't…the mating haze. I can't fight it forever, baby. Tell me no, and I'll stop. Tell me no or else this is going somewhere I'm not sure you're ready for."

But she wanted. Needed to feel something other than fear and stress. Charmeine grabbed his shoulders, pulling him down to lie on top of her. Wrapping her legs around his hips. Mammon groaned, rocking slowly. Sensually. Already showing her how much skill he had in that big body of his.

He nudged her clit hard on an upward stroke, making her gasp and tremble. Making her arch into him for more.

"Mammon."

His growl would be the death of her; the way his arms shook as he literally held himself back, the resurrection. "Tell me no, Charmeine."

"Please."

He growled louder, rocking harder, his hand sliding to her breast. Kneading and teasing. She held on to him like some sort of lifeline, desperate for more. Craving him. Wanting him to break that last bit of control he clung to. Needing him to.

"Charmeine," he growled her full name with his face nuzzled into her neck, rocking harder, still holding himself back. "I don't want to push you. Tell me no."

"I can't." Charmeine gasped as he bit her neck, scratching her nails down his back in a way that made him moan deliciously. "Please. I need to feel you. I want it."

Without another word, he yanked his shirt over his head in that guy way that made her want to moan. One hand, back of the neck, pulling the shirt and tossing it to the side. Muscles bulging, every curve and dip dancing beneath his skin. She sighed, running her hands up and down his back. Sliding along every plane, fingers tracing every hard ridge. He was just so *big*.

And so hers. "More."

"Fuck, Char." Mammon rose to his feet, dragging his pants over his hips and off his legs. Naked before her, he knelt on the edge of the bed and waited. Letting her look. Letting her need grow.

Charmeine reached for him, and he followed her request. Leaning over her body, holding his weight off of her, though. But two could tease.

She reached between them, letting her fingers trace the

curve of the head of his cock, rubbing a thumb over the precome gathered in the slit. "More."

Mammon hovered, supporting himself with one arm as he groaned and rolled into her grip, letting his lips brush hers as he whispered, "The only more is us, baby. I'm here for this. Are you?"

Without looking away, Charmeine sat up. Mammon followed, staying close, kneeling on the bed to give her room. Peering at her as if she was trying to escape, and he wanted to cage her there. Silly man.

Holding his gaze, giving him what she hoped was her sexiest smile, she pulled her dress over her head, wiggling her hips to pull the silky fabric from underneath her. Mammon sat back, his breath leaving on what sounded so much like a sigh. Watching her. Keeping his eyes on hers and his hands to himself as she revealed her body to him.

Until the dress hit the floor.

With a sigh and a groan that led straight to a growl, Mammon looked. Let his eyes wander every curve, every soft inch of her. Charmeine spread her knees wider, giving him more room, loving the way his eyes left a track of goose bumps behind. She could practically feel his stare. Could practically trace every inch he saw by the power of his gaze.

"So beautiful." His hand shook as he brought it closer, running a finger over the edge of the lace cupping her breasts. "So soft." Down to the top of her panties. Slipping a finger beneath the band, making her breath hitch. Her body shiver.

"We can leave these on." He nuzzled into her neck as his finger ran from hip bone to hip bone before sliding back up along her stomach. "I can make you come without taking them off."

Charmeine shuddered at the feel of him dragging a finger up along her breast and across her nipple, at the calculated sensuality of that touch.

"We can leave this on, too." He tugged at her bra then shook his head, looking up at her in a boyish way. His expression one that seemed so out of place and so perfect all at once. "Though I have to admit, I've been dreaming of you naked in my bed for days."

Charmeine shivered, knowing this was it. This was her time to truly acquiesce. To give him what he wanted—and to take what she simply had to have. She lifted one foot and ran it along his inner thigh. Teasing him. Brushing against where he was so hard for her as she let her growl rumble through her chest.

And then she grinned. "Reality will be better. You can take them off."

Without another word, Mammon yanked the panties down her legs. She gasped, pressing her knees together almost out of habit even as her pussy clenched in anticipation and desire. Mammon chuckled again, spreading her legs with his big hands before sliding them behind her back to unhook her bra. Before pushing her to lie back on the bed with the bulk of his body. He pulled her bra from her arms, and that, too, fell to the floor, leaving her naked and exposed. Completely vulnerable. For him. Under him.

Mammon held her gaze as he dragged his hands along the length of her body. Kept his eyes on hers as he slid a hand to one knee and pushed it down. As he opened her wide for him. As he inched back so he could see her naked and laid out just for him. As he took in every private inch of her. Every bit she'd kept hidden for so long.

"So beautiful," he whispered again, his growl making the words dark and dirty in a way they hadn't been before. Charmeine shivered, the sensation of the tension growing hotter and more primal, making her moan as well. This wasn't a man admiring something precious; this was a man about to devour something he craved. And good God, she wanted him to devour her.

"Mammon." Charmeine bit her lip as the tension in her gut tightened. As it grew. As it spread and flared hotter, became needier. "I want so much."

"I know, baby. And I'll give. I'll get you off ten different ways if you let me." He lay between her legs, his wide shoulders pushing on her thighs. "Tell me no if you want me to stop."

Charmeine groaned long and loud as he ran two thick fingers all along her. As he slid one inside when he found her so wet for him. "More."

He chuckled and pushed deeper, pressing his thumb against her clit. "Is this what you want? You want me to take? You want me to demand what I want and give you what you need?"

Charmeine shook, her body responding to his dirty words. Her heart racing. She nodded, still unable to ask. Unable to tell him what she needed but wanting so much. So, so much.

"I hear you, baby. I hear you." Mammon kissed up her thigh, teasing her. Rubbing his rough, scruffy cheek against her soft inner thigh. And he was rough. Rough and big and demanding, which was what she wanted. What she craved.

And then his mouth was on her sex, and she was gone. Every stroke of his tongue, every suckle, every press of his lips…soul-searing. She writhed, trying to move closer and escape at the same time, but his big hands held her in place. His shoulders pushing her into the mattress and holding her captive in the best possible way. In the way she needed him to…wanted him to. And Mammon didn't back off, didn't go gentle or sweet with his mouth on her. He was all hard, all aggression. He sucked and licked and spread her exactly as he wanted to until she broke, until she came with a cry of his name and an arching of her back.

He was on top of her before she came down, sliding inside her still-quivering pussy with a single stroke. No softness or teasing nudges to make sure she was ready. Mammon took what he wanted, thrust deep and claimed her pussy as his own. And she loved it.

"Fuck, baby. You're so wet." Mammon growled and bit her neck, not enough to break the skin, not a claiming bite, but enough to warn her. To make her gasp and shake. To make her want that, too. She clawed at his back, knowing she was leaving marks but not caring. He felt so good, so right. Felt as if he was made for her.

As if he knew how much she wanted him to control her in that moment, Mammon thrust harder, growling, pinning her down with his weight even as his arms circled under her shoulders to hold her closer. Restricting how she could move. Owning her. And by the fates, did she love it.

His movements were a choreographed dance of pleasure. From the harsh push inside, the slamming of his hips against hers that almost hurt, to the swivel once he'd gone deep. That little extra tease to the most delicate bits of her. He thrust and snarled and whispered filthy, filthy words to her as he held her down. As he had his way with her. As he gave her exactly what she needed. As he pushed her right over the edge.

Charmeine came again with a yelp, an inelegant sound that crept up on her just as her orgasm did. Clawing his back, wrapping her body around his to hold him deeper, she trembled through her pleasure. Riding it out. Mammon followed soon after, thrusts going off rhythm before pressing his hips in hard. He snarled and shook, filling her in a way she'd never experienced, clinging to her in a way she knew she'd never get enough of.

And oddly enough, that thought didn't scare her as much as she would have expected it to.

As they came down, as they snuggled together in a sweaty, sated pile of flesh, she rested her head against his shoulder and sighed. "I'm glad I came over."

"I'm glad, too. You should come over more often."

"Maybe I will."

He rolled onto his back, pulling her with him, forcing her to straddle his hips and lie across his chest. "Maybe I don't like maybes."

Cocky bastard. She pressed her lips to his in a slow, deep kiss. The sort of kiss that dragged on, starting over with every breath, seeming never to end. The sort of kiss that shifted, changed, and flowed until there was nothing but pressure and heat and shared breaths. The sort of kiss that spoke of emotion more than physical desire. Of longing and intimacy and…

Things she wasn't yet ready to deal with.

She pushed against his shoulder, rising to a sitting position on his hips. Mammon groaned and reached for her, pulling her tighter against him. Holding her in place for a little longer. But that was okay because he was hard again and rubbing her in all the right places. And no matter how much she knew she wasn't ready for love or trust, she was definitely ready for this. For learning each other's bodies. For lust.

She rocked over his cock, loving the way the pressure built again. The tease of it. And Charmeine liked to tease. "I should probably get going."

Mammon didn't stop, didn't even pause. He took her comment in stride, actually pressing harder against her as he pulled her hips in tighter. Making her gasp and shiver once more. Shooting her one hell of a cocky smile.

"Are you sure? I could order dinner for us and make sure you don't go home—" he thrust up, teasing her clit with the pressure of his cock "—hungry."

She couldn't have held back her groan if she'd tried. "You're a naughty boy."

That smile fell, his eyes staring into hers, his emotions on display. "For you, my mate. Only for you."

And by the fates, did she wish she could say that back. That she could find the right words to tell him that she wanted to trust him but didn't know how. That she had no idea what she was doing, but she was going to try no matter what.

But words were hard. Sex was easier…as was leaving. She leaned down again, kissing him one last time. "I really do have to go. I have work to do for the rescue, and I need to clean up first."

Mammon, though, was not a man to give up easily. "I have a shower here. I can get you clean. And I could help with the work at your rescue."

Charmeine froze. While she may have started to see Mammon as someone she could allow some access to her, the families in the rescue were not hers to risk. They had already been through so much, already had tragedy after tragedy piled high on their plates. They were—

"I don't have to." Mammon grabbed her thighs, breaking her out of her thoughts. Staring up at her. "I know how you feel about the families there. You don't have to let me in for that now. I just offered in case you needed help."

"No, I know. I just…" She paused, unsure. But her heart beat steadily, and her stomach wasn't clenched in fear or dread. At some point, she'd have to take this step. Leap off this cliff. Somewhere along the way, she'd need to bring him into her life fully and see how he fit against the world she'd created for herself. She was afraid, sure—distrusting and wary—but deep down, she wanted him with her. Wanted him to see how she spent her time. Wanted him to see her life's work in person.

Throwing caution to the wind for the first time since she could remember, she brought her hand to the side of his face and smiled. "Would you like to have a tour of the temporary living quarters? I was going to spend the day there tomorrow and thought—"

"Yes." He pulled her down for another deep kiss, holding her tight to his chest and making her moan. The kiss swirled again, lifting and growing, bites and snarls and growls replacing any sort of sweetness they'd started with.

But eventually, Mammon pulled away, breathing hard, looking up at her with lust-blown eyes. "You'd better go before I slide back inside you and make you scream."

He made his point by rocking his hips, allowing the tip of his cock to nudge inside. Just the tip. The tease. Charmeine gave as good as she got, though, rocking back against that thickness, teasing him as much as he teased her. The two pressing and retreating in a rhythm that could have brought them so much more if they'd just moved a little closer. Pushed a little harder. Let the teasing become more.

When Mammon worked a hand between them to press his thumb against her clit, sending tingles straight up her spine, Charmeine knew it was time.

She arched and sat back, pushing off his shoulders to rise to a sitting position, taking him in deep as she settled on his hips once more.

"Well, maybe I do have a few minutes."

That cocky grin on his face couldn't hide the way his eyes rolled back in pleasure. "We shouldn't waste them."

Seventeen

Mammon sent the text to Phlego and sat back against the seat, watching the world go by outside the windows. Or as much as he could with his mate sitting by his side. It was a chore to tear his eyes away from her, especially knowing how soft all that skin was. How lush those curves were. It'd been two days since Charmeine had shown up at his apartment. Forty-eight hours of texts and phone calls, but no time to see each other until he hopped in the car with her. No time with just the two of them, preferably naked and alone. Hell, even in the car, they weren't alone.

His phone vibrated with a text alert.

Nothing. Deus says they've gone silent, which could mean either they're backing off or getting ready to strike.

"Helpful, jackass."

"What's that?" Charmeine peered up at him, those blue

eyes practically piercing his heart. Mammon just shook his head and smiled until she turned back to the other person in the car. The one making Mammon's blood pressure rise. He typed out a response to his Dire brother to ignore the pounding in his head.

Keep hunting. I've got a feeling these fuckers are going for option two.

Roger that. Need extra protection?

Mammon shot a glance at Charmeine. Her hair was loose today, falling over one shoulder in a golden wave, accentuating the curve of her breast. My God, she was beautiful. And his. And she might hate him for what he was about to do, but he *would* keep her safe. No matter what.

Set it up. I'll stay with Char until we get back to the O'Rourke place. We can rendezvous there.

On it.

"Sorry, Charmeine. I missed that over all the tapping and vibrating. Can you repeat the question?" Charmeine's assistant, a little shifter by the name of Ethan, shot him a look that was somewhere between irritated and needing to take a shit. That could just have been Mammon's opinion, though.

Blood pressure…rising.

"How many properties are on the list for the permanent facility?" Charmeine asked her assistant, ignoring or flat-out not noticing the tension in the back of the car. Mammon squeezed her hand, loving that she was allowing that small bit of affection in a somewhat public forum. Well, not so much public. It was only the three of them. Mammon, Charmeine, and fucking Ethan…who kept shooting him nasty looks.

"Four. There were five, but one sold out from under us. We could have made a bid for it the day before yesterday, but…"

Ethan trailed off, his implications clear. Mammon

gripped Charmeine's hand tighter, wishing he could dress down the bratty assistant for upsetting his mate. Because she was upset. Charmeine looked as if she felt guilty, as if she hadn't deserved a night off from all her work to enjoy time with her new mate. Mammon hated that.

He hated Ethan.

There was something about the shifter that set off his wolf's need to protect and challenge, made him wary. Something that made him cranky. Not jealous in any way… but not trusting.

"Yes, well." Charmeine cleared her throat and tried to pull her hand from his. Tried to pull away from her mate because of some little shit with a Napoleon complex. That was Mammon's last straw.

"She took an afternoon off. Quit crucifying her for it." His voice was more growl than not, but Mammon didn't care. His mate was upset because of the little fucker. Ethan deserved every bit of anger he received.

The smaller shifter turned away, unable to meet Mammon's eyes. Good. Hopefully, the jackass would mind his manners next time. Mammon didn't care if the guy was super helpful to Charmeine…he wouldn't pause to put his fist in Ethan's face should the need occur.

Meanwhile, Charmeine—his sweet, kind, secretly naughty mate—smiled subtly and leaned into his shoulder. Relaxing. Craving his affection.

Mammon considered that a job well done.

The band on his wrist vibrated, and Mammon took a moment to double tap it. The guys were monitoring his location exactly as he'd requested. Again, he may have trusted Charmeine, but he certainly didn't trust the situation. Neither did his pack.

"What is that?" Charmeine asked, fingering the thick band.

"Activity tracker." The lie came without thought, and he hated himself for it. But something about being in the car with Ethan put his guard up. He would have happily told Charmeine exactly what the device on his wrist did—would have preferred if she had one on as well—but not around that other shifter. Mammon just didn't like him.

Charmeine smiled and ran those wicked fingers up his arm. "Trying to get into shape?"

"Trying?" Teasing was a new thing he loved from her, something he didn't see nearly enough in person. She was good over text, though, and they'd found a nice balance of sweetness and sour to keep their long conversations in that space lively. But in person? That wicked flirting and open smile? Totally new ball game.

Mammon grabbed her wandering hand and placed it on his leg, holding it down as he flexed his thigh. Then he leaned into her side and gave her a good growl. "Are you saying I'm not in shape?"

Charmeine bit her lip and gripped his leg, rubbing in a way that sent shock waves through his cock. "You'll hear no complaints from me."

Mammon nuzzled her neck and whispered, "Good."

But of course, Ethan had to interrupt them. "We still need to address the rest of the accounting and ordering of supplies for the next two weeks. I assume you'll be available for that, or should I contact Finn directly?"

Charmeine jerked away, shooting a glare at her assistant. "No, Ethan. I'm available. We can handle that later this morning."

Ethan glanced Mammon's way, almost looking as if he wanted a challenge. "But your guest—"

And *that* was more than enough. "I'm not her guest, and I'm not her keeper. If Charmeine has work to do, I'm sure she'll handle that. I'm her fucking mate and a grown-ass man. I can entertain myself as she takes care of business."

Ethan's face turned red, but he closed his damn mouth. Finally. And Charmeine, well, if Mammon knew her a little better, he'd say she was biting back a laugh.

Job really well done.

Eventually, the car rolled to a stop in what looked like an office complex. Long, sprawling, single-story buildings of dark brown brick sat along the parking lot. Completely bland and run-of-the-mill. Nothing to stand out, to catch attention, or even to notice as you passed by. The perfect sort of place for hiding people, in Mammon's opinion.

"We're here." Charmeine's smile lit up the interior of the car. Mammon could only stare, pieces of his mate falling into place in his mind. She loved what she did. Not just cared about her job or enjoyed helping people. She *loved* this. And he loved that grin.

Before she could step out of the car, Mammon grabbed her chin and pressed his lips to hers in a closed-mouth kiss that did nothing to quell his desire for her.

"I like this smile," he whispered when he was through. "I'd love to see more of it."

That smile grew, and Charmeine flushed. "Then come with me."

"Anywhere." He grabbed her hand and stepped out of the car, following her. Letting her lead him into her world.

Triple-tapping the tracker on his wrist to let his team know where the rescue was.

Inside, the boring building was anything but staid or plain. The hall had been painted a soft sage green color, and the fluorescent overhead lights had been left off, while lamps on tables lit the space with a golden glow. The floor was a dark vinyl of some sort, and pictures of families damn beautiful modern landscapes dotted the long expanses of wall space. Altogether, the effect was homey and comfortable.

"It's not much," Charmeine said as she walked down the hall. "But we've done the best we could with the funds and facilities available."

"Not much? This place is amazing."

Shifters crept out from doorways, looking wary until they saw Charmeine at his side. Their smiles and welcomes to her spoke more of her character than anything else could have. They trusted her, relied on her, and honestly seemed to like her. That was an amazing sight.

And then, there was Ethan…again.

"We have a call with Finn's accountant team at one, so we should probably finish up the bookkeeping that should have been completed the afternoon you took off."

Mammon growled, unable to stop himself until Charmeine placed a hand against his chest.

"Let me find Tucker so Mammon has something to do, and I'll meet you in my office."

Ethan didn't seem to like that answer, but he accepted it with a head nod before stalking down the hall.

Mammon was glad to see him leave. "He's fucking pleasant."

Charmeine snorted a laugh and pressed her forehead into his chest. "He's just protective of me."

Mammon wrapped his arm around her shoulders and pulled her tighter. "So am I."

"Miss O'Rourke." An older, male shifter with a quick step and a big smile hurried down the hall, interrupting their moment. "I hear I have a new partner in crime."

Charmeine kept her arm around Mammon's waist as she faced him. "Hi, Tucker. This is Mammon, and he'll be working with you today. Mammon, this is Tucker. He single-handedly rescued eight children from a fire the Hunters set outside of Billings a few years back. He's been a real asset to us ever since."

Mammon held out his hand, but Tucker grabbed his forearm instead, a traditional shifter greeting and a sign of respect.

"Nice to meet you, sir. And don't listen to her. She likes to brag on me a bit."

"Deservedly so, it seems," Mammon said, already liking the older shifter. "And no sirs here; Mammon is fine."

Charmeine gave his side one last squeeze. "I should get going. You'll be okay?"

"Absolutely." But as she turned to walk away, something inside of him lit up. A warning or intuition. Something that said he needed to do more. His wolf howled, and his skin itched with the need to shift. He wanted her beside him, wanted her where he could see her, smell her, save her if he needed to. He had no idea why, but something told him not to let Charmeine get out of his sights.

"Hang on." He grabbed her wrist, stopping her. With a single snap, he unclasped the tracker and latched it around her wrist instead. "If it vibrates, tap it twice. Don't forget."

Charmeine smiled down at the band. "Are you telling me I need to get into shape?"

Mammon growled and pulled her close with his hand on her ass, turning so Tucker couldn't see. "I like your shape just fine. Humor me, though."

She shot him a confused look but didn't take the band off. Mammon couldn't hold back his whimpered growls, and he was sure there was a nervousness in his eyes that she noticed. He didn't care. Let the world know he worried about his mate. They could judge him if they wanted, so long as she came home with him when the day was over.

He kissed her once. Twice. Then pulled away again. "Tap it twice every time it buzzes, okay?"

Charmeine wasn't stupid, though, and Mammon was not nearly subtle. "Mammon, what—"

"Trust me. I know you don't, but try for this one thing. Just…trust me."

She fiddled with the band but nodded, still not looking comfortable. "Fine. But I want explanations."

Yeah, he knew that was coming. "Absolutely. As soon as we leave here and get back to your place, I'll be happy to tell you anything. Now go. I have work to do, and my boss looks ready to fire my ass."

"Nah, we're good. Though if you hurt the boss lady here, you'd need to worry about me kicking, not firing, your ass." Tucker nodded to Charmeine, looking quite proud of himself. "I'll make sure he earns his keep."

"Thank you, Tucker. If you need me, I'll be in my office with Ethan."

Mammon flinched. He didn't even like hearing her say that name.

Needing a distraction from the weird, edgy feeling chasing him, Mammon let his mate go. Let her walk away. Let her do what she needed to do. Even though he hated it.

Cleaning out storerooms and building bunk beds hadn't been Mammon's favorite things about the visit to the rescue, though that was what took up the most time. No, his favorite moments had been meeting the residents there, especially some of the smaller children who snuck down the halls to get a peek at the new guy. Little shifters with big eyes and tiny hands. With shadows seeming to hover around them and scars embedded in their skin.

"They're the real victims. To die is easy—to live with the memories of what those kids saw is the hardest part," Tucker had said after one little boy ran off before Mammon could even say hi. That thought, that reality, left Mammon's heart flayed open, left him feeling raw and overwhelmed with rage and grief. Left him needing comfort in a way he'd never experienced. So the second the work was done, he left Tucker in the back bedrooms to go find his mate.

"Mister Mammon," a particularly cheeky little girl called, waving at him from the end of a hall. "Mister Finn is here, and we're going to have a puppet show. Are you coming?"

Mammon grinned. That was Emerson, the one with the burns covering one side of her face. The one who'd grabbed his hand and grinned up at him before telling him he needed to shave. She'd captured a little piece of his soul with that smile, and there was nothing he wouldn't do for her already.

"Absolutely, Emerson. But let me find Miss Charmeine first so she can watch it, too."

"Okay!" Emerson raced back into the room, blond pigtails streaking behind her.

"She'd better not ever ask for a pony," Mammon whispered to himself as he started back down the hall. "Because I'll buy a whole damn stable for her."

The building Charmeine rented for her refugees sprawled with multiple hallways leading off in cross patterns every so many feet. It was a confusing space, one easy to get turned around in, but Mammon was pretty sure where he should be going.

That was, until he saw Ethan standing down a darkened hallway he knew wasn't the right one.

"Ethan?"

The shifter jerked back, his eyes wide as he stared at Mammon. As he looked about in what certainly seemed like a panic. Mammon's wolf roared, and his instincts flared again. Something wasn't right.

"Where's Charmeine?"

But Ethan didn't answer. Instead, he turned and strode the other way. Trying to escape or avoid. Either way, that shit wasn't happening. Mammon followed on instinct alone, catching up slowly. Choosing not to overrun the little fucker in case one of the kids came down this way. But before Mammon could grab him, Ethan reached the end of the hall and turned, shoving open a set of fire doors.

"Shit." Kids be damned, Mammon gave chase. He hit the fire doors before they could close behind the fleeing Ethan, pushing them back open with a snarl of rage. The shifter, the black SUV, the tiny, hidden parking lot, none of it mattered because as soon as he stepped outside, his stomach dropped into his shoes.

Fear.

Charmeine's scent was everywhere in the little parking lot outside the door, and it was tinged with fear. His mate was in danger and afraid.

"Charmeine!"

But an explosion from behind him sent the Dire to his knees before he could take more than a single step. Concrete tore his pants and scraped his palms, but that wouldn't stop him. The kids…his mate. He needed to save them all. It took way more strength and focus than was normal, a sign the blast had done something worse to him than a simple fall, but eventually he was able to crawl forward. To compel his body into action. He had just pushed himself to his feet when a second blast rocked the world around him. The force sent him sprawling, his head making contact with the pavement before any other part of him. The sound of something coming closer, a rhythm much like running footsteps, only made his head ache that much more. Mind fading as a pain unlike any he'd experienced wrapped around him, he almost missed the sight of a pair of white shoes coming closer.

Shoes…not boots. *Shit.*

Eighteen

"Mammon needs you."

Charmeine looked up from the spreadsheet she'd been reviewing to find her assistant leaning in the door. "Is everything okay?"

"I assume, but Tucker asked me to grab you. Said your friend needed you for something."

Charmeine bristled, unable not to. "He's my mate, not just my friend."

Ethan's lip curled, and his eyes seemed to harden right in front of her. Fury. That expression reminded Charmeine of pure, unadulterated fury. But a moment later, it was gone, and Ethan was back to being his very bland, very docile self.

"Yes, I'm aware. I wasn't sure if you were telling all the refugees yet, though."

Run.

Charmeine's instincts flared, her highly tuned sense of survival kicking in out of nowhere. But she didn't run, she didn't even walk. She waited, analyzing, running her fingers over the edge of the band Mammon had put on her wrist. She was tired from staring at numbers all day; that was what was going on. Ethan was her cousin, had been her friend and confidant for decades. Maybe he was jealous or overworked and that was why this mating bothered him. Or maybe he didn't like Mammon—a definite possibility. Mammon certainly seemed not to like the smaller shifter. Either way, this was not a life-or-death moment.

"Thank you for coming to let me know," Charmeine said as she grabbed her paperwork, her voice quieter than she would have liked.

Ethan stared for a moment, then he nodded once. "Of course. Though I don't think you'll need all that stuff."

"Yes, you're probably right." Charmeine clutched at the printouts, talking her heart into beating a normal, slower rhythm, before placing them neatly back on the table. Maybe she needed a break. She wasn't done working yet, but it was later in the afternoon than she'd originally thought. She couldn't blame Mammon for being ready to leave, if that was what this was. So she followed Ethan out the door and down the hall, fiddling with the band around her wrist. She'd been tapping it twice every time it vibrated as Mammon had instructed, even though she'd already figured out it couldn't be an activity tracker and there was no face for a watch. That was something she'd deal with later, though. After they were alone.

Ethan turned down a hallway they hadn't updated yet, one without proper lighting. The walls were still a weird pistachio color, and the dirty carpet carried a slight mildew scent. This was not where Mammon was supposed to be working.

"What are we doing down here?" Charmeine asked as they reached a set of fire doors at the end.

"I'm just following orders." Ethan knocked twice and

stepped aside, farther away from the entrance.

When the door opened, Charmeine didn't have time to run. She didn't even have time to scream. Two men rushed in and grabbed her, dragging her outside. One clamped his hand over her mouth and held her wrists behind her back. The other practically lifted her off the ground. There was no fighting them, no escaping them. No way out. But that wasn't going to stop her from trying.

"Quit fighting," one man said as she kicked and attempted to throw her body weight around. "You don't want to be inside, considering what's coming."

Charmeine froze, panic an icy wave that stole her breath. The children. The families. Mammon. Even Ethan didn't seem to be outside with her, which meant he was still in the building.

The men shoved her into the back of a dark SUV. She kicked and fought harder, biting the hand on her mouth and screaming as loud as she could. The men didn't stop, though. They pushed and shoved, growling, forcing her through the door and deep into the rear passenger area. But they didn't cover her mouth again.

Charmeine growled, letting her wolf come forward more than she had in months. "Where are you taking me?"

One of the men who'd grabbed her, the man who'd sat in the front seat, snorted what sounded like a laugh, as if her question didn't matter. As if she didn't matter. The second man jumped in the back through the same door Charmeine had been forced through, followed by…

"Ethan." Charmeine nearly cried in frustration and rage. "What are you doing?"

The man she'd called family, whom she'd treated as a friend, looked at her with eyes so cold and evil, Charmeine could only recoil.

"I'm following orders, remember?"

"I thought you meant Tucker's orders. You…you're working for the Hunters?" Charmeine's eyes blurred, and she could only shake her head. "You sold us out."

"I did what I needed to do to stay alive."

"We would have helped if you'd told us they approached you. Finn and I—"

"You being involved would have been a death sentence for my family," he said, interrupting her. "You try and try and try, but shifters keep dying. You may as well be a murderer."

"No," Charmeine gasped, shaking her head. Refusing to believe those harsh words. "We keep them safe. We give them opportunities for a life not made up solely of running."

Ethan sneered, his eyes filling with hate. "You cost them their lives. But the Apex Hunters will keep me safe now that I've delivered their biggest desire—the cherry on the top of the Byrne sundae."

Charmeine shook her head, trying so hard not to cry. Ethan was family; he wasn't supposed to do this. He wasn't supposed to put everyone she cared about in danger. And he certainly wasn't supposed to have sold her to the enemy.

But he had, and he'd done it right under her nose.

As the car pulled away, leaving the little parking lot behind, an explosion rattled the windows and rocked the heavy SUV. Charmeine screamed and ducked, searching out the windows for the source. Knowing what she'd see before she spotted it.

A plume of black smoke rose from the far side of the rescue building. Fire.

Charmeine lunged for the door, thinking of the children and adults, of Mammon and little Emerson. Of all the death that could have been avoided had Ethan stayed loyal. Had she noticed his betrayal sooner. Had she done something to help them.

The guard shoved her back into a seat without care for

the losses they were leaving behind. A second explosion blasted through the air as they left the complex, and then they were flying down the road. No way out, no way to help. No way to survive.

"How could you?" Charmeine asked, staring right at Ethan. "You're my family."

"But not Byrne family, which is all that really seemed to matter to you. You never talked about your mom's family, about my parents or cousins. It was all about the high and mighty Byrnes in your world. So, no, Charmeine. You're not family to me. You never have been." He had the audacity to shrug. "Besides, someone needed to knock you and Finn down a peg or two."

Charmeine couldn't even feel sorry for herself. She was too mad, too angry at him to think about the loss of someone she'd considered a friend. "So this is about your ego? You set up our family and friends to be murdered so you could feel more important?"

Ethan growled, low but vicious. "No, I did it to stay alive."

"What about the children?"

"It's every family for themselves right now." Ethan turned to stare out the side window as the car hit the highway. "Besides, the Apex Hunters promised they wouldn't hurt the children."

If those words hadn't been so wrong, she might have laughed. "Oh, Ethan. Do you really believe them?"

The guard she'd almost forgotten about slapped her hard, knocking her to the floor. "Shut the fuck up, Byrne whore. Your fate is sealed. As is the fate of everyone who chose to participate in your so-called rescue mission."

Charmeine crawled back onto the seat, biting back tears. She was trapped, the people she'd been trying to help possibly dead, and her mate missing with them. She didn't know what to do next or how long it would take someone to realize she was even missing in the chaos of what had to be happening back at the rescue.

Suddenly, she regretted not exchanging mating bites with Mammon. If they had, he could feel her fear. He could sense where she was. He could find her, just as she could have found him. They'd know the other was at least alive. But she'd resisted the draw that day in his apartment, had chosen to keep that wall in place, and now she was alone and fighting for her life.

Mammon's activity tracker vibrated on her wrist, reminding her of his intensity when he gave it to her. Of his care. She rubbed it but, against his wishes, didn't tap it twice. Why bother? She'd probably be dead within a few hours.

Nineteen

Cold. The sensation roused Mammon, soaking into his body in a way that made his joints and muscles ache. Even before he opened his eyes, he could feel the dampness in the air. The wet, old smell around him that he couldn't place. Something was very, very wrong.

He opened one eye, too exhausted and sore to handle both at once. Pain stabbed through his head, throwing his thoughts into disarray. He cringed but held back his growl. Deep breaths and balls of steel, that's what gave him the courage to try again. One eye, slowly. Barely a slit. Better, not in a *hey, everything's cool* sort of way. More in an *at least nothing's stabbing me in the brain* way. He'd take it.

Mammon blinked, risking both eyes, unsure if his battered brain was playing tricks on him or not. Stone floor… dark room…no windows…tiny light from under a closed and probably locked door. Trapped and alone in a strange place. Okay. So, something was definitely wrong and in a not-good sort of way. He closed his eyes, ignoring the cold and the ache it caused, focusing on getting his brain to work properly. The more he came to, the more memories flooded back. The rescue, Charmeine's smile, Tucker, Emerson…the blasts that knocked him out.

Shit.

Thoughts of the rescue were the only things clear in his mind. His desire to find the people who'd been inside the building, to make sure the kids and parents were all right, fueled every inch of Mammon and gave him the strength to lift his upper body from the floor. He wobbled but didn't fall over. Definitely a good sign. He'd been through blasts before—it was going to suck, but he needed to be vertical. Get his blood flowing and give his brain a chance to catch back up. He groaned as he pushed to his knees, though. Motherfucking explosions, they always made him feel as if he'd been hit by a truck. Not that he'd been hit by a truck before, but he had to imagine the deep, throbbing ache the force of a blast left behind felt similar. Still, he pushed past all that. He had to.

Charmeine. Tucker. Emerson. Finn.

Mammon needed to fight the pain and confusion dragging him down. He needed to figure out where he was and how to get out. Already, his wolf paced in his mind, anguished but furious that someone would dare to attack a Dire Wolf. There was also the fact that his mate had been inside the building; she was definitely in danger either from the explosions or the attackers. His wolf snarled and dropped his head in a threatening posture, ready to go to war. Ready to take over and raze anyone and anything that got in his way of finding Charmeine. She was his priority, his focus, his sole responsibility.

God save anyone who put a hand on her.

What felt like hours later, after staring at the door he'd made sure was locked and definitely too thick to kick down, footsteps approached. Mammon sat against the opposite wall, legs straight out and crossed at the ankles. Deceptively casual. All confusion and pain from the blasts were gone, all control over his rage decimated. He wasn't resting—he was preparing for battle.

When the door swung open, five armed men stormed in and stood in a formation. Mammon didn't even blink, too busy thinking tactics to entertain the fuckers. He could handle five standard shifters in a fight, but he'd need to get rid of the guns. He'd been shot on the last mission with Levi, and he didn't feel like dealing with that again. So guns first, then guards. If they were all Apex Hunters, as he assumed they were, then most if not all were in this place he was being held. An assumed pack of no more than ten, Finn had said. Mammon liked the idea of taking them all out at once like bowling pins. And though he was technically the prisoner, he'd figure out a way to throw a strike. That was the Dire way.

A sixth man walked in after the advance squad secured the room. Mammon could have rolled his eyes at that thought. Secure in their world meant making a show of their guns, apparently. No one had actually checked on him to see if he had somehow armed himself. No one had secured him to the wall or floor. Amateurs, this lot. That would definitely work in his favor.

The sixth man walked in as if he owned the place—and maybe he did. The shifter stood tall, his posture perfect, his haughty sneer probably practiced in a mirror. Someone posing as a leader or a warrior without the proper knowledge to back themselves up. Arrogance without skill was so easy to spot.

Mammon kept his spot on the floor and simply raised an eyebrow. "You really think six will contain me? Well, five—somehow I doubt you'd get your hands dirty in a fight."

The leader's lips curled up in an oily sort of smile. "You're quite cocky considering the situation."

Mammon snorted. At least *he* had the knowledge to back up his attitude.

"I prefer confident." Mammon cocked his head, knowing he was about to give away a bit more than he wanted but needing the info. "Where're the people from the rescue?"

"They're here." Arrogance personified smirked—*motherfucking smirked*—before lifting a shoulder in a forced-casual sort of way. "Most of them, at least. I mean, we did blow that hovel pretty hard."

Mammon held his position, biting back a growl so hard, his jaw ached. He couldn't show his hand, but he needed to know about his mate. Was desperate for her. Without a mating bite, he couldn't sense her. Had he bitten her, had they exchanged bites during sex, he would be able to pinpoint her location and track her down. And then the devil himself would have been the only man who could have saved her captors. But they hadn't exchanged bites, so he was left with only his normal senses, which weren't exactly firing on all cylinders quite yet. Goddamned explosions.

Mammon crossed his arms over his chest, still trying to keep his cool, the movement forcing him to notice his wrist. His very bare wrist that made a lightbulb go off in his mind. So he had his normal senses and Deus' non-normal tracking device. He'd put it on Charmeine's wrist at the rescue, had made a mental note to tell her what it was once they had a moment alone together. As long as she wore that, his brothers could find her. When she didn't tap in response to their vibration, they'd assume something was wrong with Mammon and come running. Because she wore it, they'd find her. A terrifying thought, sort of. He could only hope Phego was one of the men working the extraction team—the rest had never met her and would probably scare the life right out of her. But at least they'd come. His Dire family would be here, and they'd save her. One worry taken off his plate.

"Your mate is alive, if that's your concern," Arrogance said.

Mammon froze, meeting the man's eyes. Knowing he was fucked. "I don't know what you're talking about."

Those eyebrows went up in an exaggerated fashion that made Mammon's blood turn cold. "Oh, now, let's not be coy." He turned to his guards and nodded. One stepped out into the hall, but it was the sound of two sets of footsteps coming back that made Mammon sit up. Oh God, Charmeine? Was she here, so close, and he hadn't sensed her? He couldn't smell her, but—

When the guard came back with Ethan at his side, Mammon's world went red with fury. There was no controlling his wolf's growl, no holding back the threat in his voice.

"How much?" he asked, letting his snarl come through his words.

Ethan stared at him, not speaking. Almost hiding behind the five soon-to-be-dead guards and their leader who all blocked Mammon's escape path.

But Mammon rejected Ethan's silence. "How much was her life worth to you? Finn's? Those kids'?"

Ethan licked his lip and glanced at Arrogant. "The children were not to be harmed."

Mammon's forced laugh hurt; it physically made him ache in ways he hated. Little feet under pink skirts, ponytails bouncing, and gap-toothed smiles flashed before his eyes. He knew those kids, had met them and played with them at the rescue. After just one day, he'd cared for them. This fucker had known them for weeks and sold them out for…what?

"You're an idiot to have believed that." Mammon shook his head, fighting back the need to tear everyone in the room apart limb from limb. "Tell him, Mister Leader Man. Tell him the truth this time."

Arrogant glared until Ethan looked his way, but then he shrugged. Pretending to be casual again. "There is always collateral damage in any mission."

Ethan's shocked face would have been funny had the cause not been so fucking horrifying.

The traitor began to whine and question the leader in his presumptuous way, but Mammon had better things to focus on. Like the vibration coming through the floor. It was subtle, but there. Something coming closer. Something the others couldn't feel as they stood a few feet away. But Mammon could. He felt the thundering steps of what he knew had to be his brothers through the stone floor, felt them in his thighs and in his heart. His pack was coming for him, and they were not men to be messed with.

Mammon pushed off the stone, slowly rising to his feet. The guards all took a step back, and Arrogant quit proffering excuses to watch. Mammon's joints still hurt, and the ache of knowing there could be dead children back at the rescue made breathing harder than he would have liked, but he stood. And he growled. And he glared down at Arrogant with every ounce of hatred he'd ever possessed.

The floor vibrated to the point he could feel it through his bare feet. Mammon leaned a shoulder against the wall, the picture of calm, cool, and motherfucking collected. "Collateral damage… I'm sort of digging that term."

Arrogant shot him a nasty look, but Mammon could only smirk in return. One by one, the guards perked up, swiveling their heads toward the door, looking for something not quite there yet. Mammon was no longer the only one who could feel the approaching storm. Three guards turned around as vibrations turned to footsteps. Then a fourth. And still, the sound grew louder. Closer.

Mammon was almost giddy. "I think it's time for a little collateral damage of my own."

He jumped on Arrogant just as Phego and Bez rushed in the door. And then Thaus barreled his way through with a roar that shook the foundation. Mammon had one moment of *what-the-fuck*, because Thaus was fighting like a man possessed, before he ignored his brothers to focus on his prey. Arrogant barely fought back, too overwhelmed by the whirling dervish Mammon had become to do more than cry out for help. But his guards were too busy handling the other Dires. Or being slaughtered by them, really. When a team was as trained and skilled as the Dires, dispatching half-assed guards took little time, so it was only a few minutes later that Mammon raced out the door and into the hallway, his Dire brothers on his heels.

"Plan?" Thaus asked, looking positively feral with blood dripping down his chin and onto his shirt.

"Guards all gone?"

Phego chimed in from his place trailing the others. "Five down plus your target."

Mammon wanted to scream. "Five plus mine means Ethan got away. Fucking traitor must have run the second you three arrived. I'm taking him out."

Still running, Mammon glanced back at Thaus. At the man who helped keep all the Dires on task. The one with the worst attitude, the strongest temper, and the scariest personality outside of the beast known as Luc. The one he trusted more than anything or anyone. "My mate is in here somewhere."

Thaus didn't seem to be surprised. "Tell me what you need."

"I'll handle the traitor named Ethan. You find my mate."

Thaus gave him a nod before turning down a different hallway, shifting on the fly as he did. Shit, Charmeine was going to be terrified of that thing coming to get her. Mammon faltered, wanting to follow Thaus, needing to see Charmeine, but there was still danger. Five, maybe six Apex Hunters down meant there were possibly four more. The NALB had failed the first time they'd dispatched that crew—Mammon wouldn't let them fail this time.

"Bez," he called, slowing at a convergence of hallways to figure out a direction. "Possible four targets remain."

"On it." Bez took off down a dark hallway, probably following his nose to where he'd find more of the Hunters. Which was good, but Mammon had a different job to do.

Mammon followed Ethan's scent down a different hallway and out a door at the end of some dark, wet space. As he walked up the three steps to the grassy lawn, he spotted the little fucker racing away. Ethan glanced behind him, his eyes going wide when he spotted Mammon so close. Had he taken the time, Mammon would have smiled and waved. A nice warning that he was coming for the little traitor. Instead, he took off at a run.

Ethan picked up his pace before shifting to his wolf form, probably thinking four legs were faster than two. And they were, but Mammon had four legs as well, and his legs were longer, stronger, and faster than any non-Dire wolf he'd ever come across.

Mammon shifted in midstep, letting his wolf take over the hunt. Faster, harder, his wolf stretched out every stride, dug for grip on every pawfall. Pictures of his mate and Tucker and little Emerson fueling a rage too strong to contain.

Mammon caught up to Ethan fast, grabbing the fleeing wolf's ankle on a forward stride and flipping him to his back. And then he attacked. Family or no family, Ethan was a traitor. He'd sold out Charmeine, put the children of the rescue in danger, and destroyed the lives of those living within. He deserved no judge, no jury, and no stay of execution.

Teeth and claws sliced the weaker flesh, quickly dispatching the shifter. Mammon wished the fight could have lasted longer. He wanted Ethan to suffer, to hurt the way he'd hurt Charmeine. To feel the agony of a slow, savage death as he deserved. But there was more at stake with this mission. More people to find. More lives at risk.

So a quick but messy death it was.

When the assistant lay dead at his paws, Mammon shifted human again. Naked and covered in filth, he ran back toward the house once more. Phego ran beside him, having apparently been watching the whole time. Backing Mammon up but letting him have the kill.

"Charmeine?" Phego asked, the one word striking dread in Mammon's heart. Still, though, he shook his head.

"No, we need to find the children from the rescue if they're here, and I have a feeling they are."

Phego stumbled, staring at him. "What?"

"I sent Thaus for my mate. If anyone can find her and keep her safe, it's him. But Charmeine will never forgive herself if those kids are hurt, and I'll never forgive myself if I don't try to find them right away."

"There are still Hunters at large."

Mammon wanted to snarl, but he couldn't. He had to focus. "Bez is on it. Six down, four to go. But there's a little blond girl with a stuffed wolf who wanted me to watch her puppet show, and damn it, I'm going to watch it."

Phego caught up, running by Mammon's side as they reached the stone house they'd come out of only moments before. As they ran right back into the hell Mammon had woken up in.

"Kids it is, then."

The noises outside Charmeine's cell grew louder and more violent as the minutes passed. She had no idea what to do, though. She was trapped, locked in some sort of basement with no way out. So she paced, and she rubbed the activity tracker thing Mammon had given her. And she worried about everyone. Finn, who was supposed to be at the rescue, her friends, the families she felt responsible for… her mate.

"Please, Mammon." She rubbed her wrist again as the band vibrated. The thing had been vibrating at an increased frequency since she stopped tapping it. There was a pattern to it, almost a code-like repetition, though she had no clue what it all meant. Still, the band was obviously not what she'd thought, and if she ever saw Mammon alive again, he was going to have some serious explaining to do. Right after she kissed him until she couldn't breathe.

The heavy thunk of the door being unlocked stopped her in her tracks. Her time was up. She turned, holding her head high, her wolf ready to take over at any moment. Because deep down, Charmeine knew there was no getting out of here without some sort of fight.

A guard walked in, tall and scarred in ways most wolves weren't. He incited fear, though she couldn't tell if that was instinctual to her wolf or if it was something else. Something bigger coming. The sense of dread in the air that seemed to press in on her, to suffocate her.

The man smiled at her in a way that turned her blood to ice. "Time's up, princess."

Fear trickled down her spine in an icy rivulet, but she wouldn't give in to it. Couldn't. She had people to protect and a mate to find. A man who cared for her, who she felt safe with, who she needed beside her. The very thought of Mammon gave her strength and ramped up her courage. He would fight for her, so she would fight for him.

Mask in place, every bit of pride she'd learned in her long life keeping her back straight, she ran a single finger over the band around her wrist and answered as she knew her mate would.

"Fuck you."

The guard chuckled, a low, raspy sound that almost made her shiver. "Such a dirty mouth. Too bad you never had the chance to use it properly." He stepped closer, moving smoothly, staring at her the entire time. Hunting her. "Or maybe you do."

Charmeine called to her wolf. The beast jumped forward, growling so loudly, the echo bounced back. "I'd rather die."

He shrugged. "Already happening. You *and* all those animals you had holed up in that slum."

"No." Charmeine's whispered reply was unstoppable, something that came right from her heart. The families she'd worked so hard to save, the children she'd cared for… Mammon. All gone if this shifter was correct. Or soon to be.

"Oh, yes," her captor said. "It's time to exterminate a few families, starting with the Byrnes and the O'Rourkes."

He reached behind his back and pulled out a gun. An honest to God gun. Something she'd never come face-to-face with before. Charmeine couldn't move, knowing one shot to the head would end her right there. Scared, but not ready to surrender just yet. She needed to think, to run, to get past him. She needed to figure out a way to escape before he—

A huge wolf rushed into the room with a snarl and leaped on top of her captor. The wolf didn't look like Mammon— her mate was a lighter color than this beast with more spots along his head—but he was big and spotted in the way of the Dire Wolf. One of Mammon's brothers, she assumed. And Charmeine had never been so happy to be forced to watch violence in all her life.

Okay, so happy was the wrong word.

She kept her eyes on the floor and inched toward the door as the worst of the fight turned bloody. She couldn't watch, didn't want to be sick from the sounds and the gore. She wouldn't try to stop it, though. There was a chance Mammon had sent the larger shifter, but she couldn't witness his decimation of the guard. Not without vomiting in a corner and embarrassing herself. Embarrassing her mate. She would be strong for him even though the scent of blood on the air made her stomach roll and her breath catch. Strong as she worked her way toward an escape so she could find out what had happened to the rest of the people at the shelter.

Before she could reach the exit, though, the fight ended. No more growling or snarling. The only sounds in the room were the heavy breaths of two beings. Her, and…

Holy shit.

When she peeked to see who had won the fight, she began to shake in fear. The wolf, now a man, stood naked and panting, a huge, hulking form with cropped hair and light eyes. There was something so dark about him, so plainly rage-filled and almost evil. An air of malevolence that soured everything around him. He may have been Mammon's brother, but he scared her. A lot.

"Come." His barked order pounded into her chest, and her wolf responded. Wanting to follow him. Sensing something more than her human side did.

Yet she resisted. "I don't know you."

"Come with me, or die."

Her wolf whined, and the man cocked his head. As if he knew. As if he could hear her inner wolf, which was impossible.

Charmeine stiffened her shoulders and lifted her chin, trying so hard not to quake in fear. "Where's Mammon?"

The man's lips turned up at one corner, a cocky sort of smile forming. "The fates chose well—a stubborn mate for my most stubborn brother."

"I prefer to think of myself as tenacious, and right now, I'm holding on to the fact that I don't know anything about you."

He chuckled, the sound dark and grating. "I am a Dire Wolf like your mate, young one. You can trust me. I will take you to Mammon."

"I trust no one."

He tilted his head, an animal appraising her through human eyes. A disturbing thought for sure. But Charmeine stood her ground as he stalked closer. As he reached for her. As he grabbed her arm and lifted. As he tugged on the band around her wrist.

"Your mate gave you this so we could track you. That's why it vibrates. It's Dire Deus checking in and sending coded messages so Mammon knows what to expect."

Charmeine stared at the black band, her heart breaking. "He knew the Hunters were coming? That the rescue center would be attacked?"

"No." The man's single word made her jerk, made her look up in surprise to meet his uncomfortable stare. God, what was inside this man that made him seem so…wrong?

"No?" she asked, all breathy and weak.

"Mammon didn't know, and neither did the rest of us. He worried about his mate, though, so he gave her the one thing he knew we'd come after. Himself. We never leave a brother behind, and no Dire fights alone if they don't have to. So he gave you this to protect you because he cares." He crowded her, leaning over her smaller body in a way that was pure threat, his voice more growl than not. "And when we found him here—because even without this piece of plastic, I know where my brothers are—Mammon asked for help from me to get you out. Don't make me go back and tell him I had to leave you behind."

Charmeine swallowed hard, the cold from his touch creeping up her arm. "You wouldn't."

He smiled…sort of. His face turning up in an expression that sent chills all the way to her toes. "You're right. I'd just throw you over my shoulder and force you to come with me. Or I could shift wolf and Alpha order you. Either way, you and I are leaving this room together. You choose the how."

"I…" Charmeine didn't know what to say. She wanted to go with him, to find Mammon. To leave this place. But she was scared. Almost her entire life, she'd been scared. She had no idea how to move past it.

Before she could find her words, the man turned, heading for the door. "Sometimes you have to act on faith. Just like how we acted on faith by coming here when Mammon didn't tap that band."

"Where are you going?"

"To find Mammon. He was after the man who betrayed you, and he may need my help." He glanced over his shoulder, his eyes hard. "You coming?"

Charmeine stood in place for a long moment, listening to the man's footsteps grow farther away. She wanted to go, needed to find her mate and any survivors from the rescue, but she felt frozen. Locked in her own fears and doubts. *Mammon, Mammon, Mammon,* she chanted in her mind. She closed her eyes, picturing him beckoning her. Waiting for her.

She pictured him searching for her.

She was at the door before she truly grasped what she was doing, running down the hall in pursuit of the darker Dire Wolf before she could stop herself. She needed to move forward, and this was the first step. Putting faith in someone to lead her out of this hell. Even if that person scared her.

"Good call, princess," the man grumbled as she caught up to him.

"I'm not a princess."

"Could have fooled me."

His arrogance made him less scary at least. "I still don't trust you."

"That's fine. I don't trust you much, either."

"Then why are you rescuing me?"

"Because you're his mate, which makes you family." The man's eyes glowed, an inhuman light shining into the dark space. "I will never leave a member of my family behind."

He shoved open a door that led out of the building. Her heart soared at the picture across the grass—Phego and another large man she didn't recognize but knew had to be a Dire Wolf shifter were lining up families from the rescue on the rolling lawn. Finn ran from group to group, counting, checking in with them. Verifying everyone had made it out of the rescue just as she would have done had she not been held up inside. She could have cried. But still, she searched the crowd, not ready to relax. Needing to find...

No Mammon. No Tucker or Ethan. Incomplete families standing together looking at the building behind her with tears in their eyes. And that's when it hit her…

None of the refugee children was outside with the others. Not a single one.

And her heart shattered in her chest. "Oh, no."

The Dire Wolf at her side looked down at her in confusion, but before she could explain, he jerked into a hunting crouch. With one swipe, he shoved her behind him, snarling viciously at the approaching shifter. Charmeine reached out to touch the Dire's arm, to stay his ire as Finn hurried over.

"It's okay," she whispered, grateful for his protection even though it was unnecessary.

He didn't relax, though. "You sure you know him?"

She nodded, her eyes burning with unshed tears. "He might as well be my brother."

Finn hurried to her side, giving the Dire a wide berth. "Jesus, I'm so glad to see you. Are you okay?"

Charmeine melted into his hug, needing someone else to hold her up for just a moment. "I'm fine. But the rest…"

Even though she couldn't finish her sentence, Finn seemed to understand what she wanted to say. What she needed to know.

"So far, only two losses at the rescue," he said. "We think there are still people inside here, though. There's a search underway."

Charmeine buried her fears under details, pulling threads together to make a picture she could trace. "What about the Apex Hunters?"

"Definite six of ten Hunters confirmed dead," Finn said.

"Seven," the Dire at her side said, not looking at either of them but instead staring at another basement door across the hill. "I took one down personally."

"Ten." Another man ran up, naked and almost completely covered in blood with light eyes and a look about him that spoke of horrible things. "Mammon sent me to find the rest, and I took out three in that labyrinth of a basement."

But Charmeine couldn't think of numbers or stone passages, she was too caught up on a specific word the man had spoken. "Mammon?"

The Dire who'd rescued her caught her eye, nodding toward the door he'd been watching. "There. Patience."

Charmeine stared at the door across the way, waiting for what felt like hours. But all that frustration, all that fear, disappeared the second the door opened. Her entire world righted itself as Mammon strode out of the basement of the house. Wearing cargo pants that looked as if they were meant for a much shorter man, he carried a child on each hip. Emerson on the left in her little pink shorts and her blond pigtails, and a little boy of barely a year on the right. Three children followed behind him as if he was the pied piper. As if he was their savior. And perhaps he was.

Every child of the rescue had survived.

Charmeine couldn't control herself a moment longer. She took off at a run, racing across the grass toward her mate. He spotted her before she reached him and set the children down so he could sweep her off her feet and into his arms.

Home. Safe. Love.

"Thank the fates." He pulled her tight, cradling her head and nuzzling into her neck. "Thaus found you."

"Is that his name? I didn't ask."

Mammon tensed, pulling away, staring at her with a peculiar look on his face. "You went with him without asking who he was?"

Charmeine shrugged, her lips turning up. "He said he was your family, which kind of makes him mine. I took a leap of faith."

Mammon grinned. "A huge leap."

She laughed and melted into him, pressing her lips to his in a kiss of thanks and relief. He'd made it, they'd almost all made it. And though they would mourn the refugees lost to another Apex Hunters' attack, the end of their long, fearful journey was close to the end. The Dires had killed all ten Hunters. The threat was over.

Or so she hoped.

Mammon groaned as he ended the kiss, licking his lips and staring into her eyes. "Dire Wolf families are forever, you know."

Charmeine grinned and pulled him closer, needing those lips again. Ready and willing to take another leap so long as he was by her side. "Sounds good to me."

Epilogue

This blue isn't really working for me." Mammon frowned at the wall. Was it too blue? Too green? Shit, he wasn't an interior designer by any stretch, but something about the shade didn't work for him.

"Then I guess it's a good thing you won't be sleeping in this room." Charmeine pushed her pole higher, slowly painting all the way up to the trim line he'd cautiously cut in before they moved on to the rollers.

"True. I just wonder if the boys will like it."

"They'll like it."

But still, he doubted. "How do you know? Maybe they'd like a gray more. Or black. Boys like black."

"We're not painting a room for children black." Charmeine gawked at him, staring as if he'd grown two heads or something. Not exactly the expression he was going for, but he had her attention. Which was always what he wanted.

It took work not to grin at his mate. "No, really. I think black would be amazing."

Irritation flashed across her pretty face. "Mammon."

Jesus, he loved it when she said his name. Even if the word was tinged with frustration. Especially then, which was why he loved pushing her buttons so much.

"We'd never have to clean the walls." At her exasperated sigh, Mammon dropped his roller and stalked across the room, grabbing her by the hips and pulling her against him. Needing contact. Craving it. "Boys are pretty dirty."

"You're pretty dirty," Charmeine mumbled.

Yes. Yes, he was. Only for her, though. And thank fuck, she was just as dirty for him. It'd been a rough month since the bombing. The Dire Wolves had taken to patrolling the rescue building—well, what was left of it. Everyone had been moved into the four rooms that could contain them, but no rebuilding had begun. Charmeine focused all her time on finding a new place, a piece of property with a big house where they could all live as a pack. What had once been Ethan's job became hers. She attacked every task with gusto, and she succeeded faster than any of them expected.

The farmhouse they stood in had once been home to a family of German immigrants who'd taken their chances on the oceans, then moved south looking for prosperity in the land. Left abandoned for a number of years, the old house had begun to fall apart and show her age. But Charmeine had seen the possibilities, especially as the land the house sat on backed up to a large area ripe with wildlife and open places to run. Perfect for wolves.

Once Charmeine signed on the dotted line of the deed—they could all thank Finn for that hefty donation— the repairs began. Every Dire Wolf jumped in, every refugee coming to help as well. A family unit working together for one goal. They'd polished and shined, repaired broken drywall and leaky pipes. Rewired everything and made sure the entire house was up to code, alarmed, and ready to defend. Just in case.

All that was left were the final touches—a little paint, some added trim, and a few doorknobs. They were almost done, which was good because the refugees would be moving over in the next day or two.

Which reminded him…

Mammon grabbed his roller and pointed it at the wall. "Paint harder. There are people coming soon."

Charmeine gaped at him. "How on earth does one paint harder?"

He couldn't resist that face. Couldn't stop teasing her if he tried.

"Like this." Mammon grabbed a paintbrush and patted it against her nose. Her eyes went wide, and her mouth dropped open. It was a shocked look, but it fucking turned him on. Something about her lips parted like that. About that sexy-as-sin mouth he couldn't get enough of.

"Damn, you're so beautiful," he murmured, letting his growl rumble over his words. But then he grinned. "Even with paint on your nose."

Her lips quirked into a smile, though she tried to stay calm and cool. "You, sir, are a filthy beast."

"And you, ma'am, love me in all my filthy beast ways."

He dropped his brush and grabbed his mate, holding her close. Squeezing her ass under her soft, cotton skirt as he lifted her. Pressing her hips against where he was so hard for her. Always.

Charmeine melted into his hold, releasing a noise so much like a purr, it made his cock twitch. "I do love your filthy beast ways."

Mammon growled, finding an unpainted wall to push her against so he could get more leverage. "We're alone, my mate."

Charmeine rocked against him, definitely on board with

where his thoughts had gone. "Such a rare occurrence these days."

"And about to be rarer once all the refugees move in."

She bit her lip, slowing her movements. Looking at him with something close to worry in her eyes. "You know you don't have to move all the way out here."

Mammon fought not to roll his eyes. This had been an argument since he'd made the decision to move in with the refugees. And with his mate. She worried and hedged, making sure not to push. Always questioning if the move was something he truly wanted. As if she didn't think he was serious. As if she didn't realize how far he would go to keep her at his side. A move was nothing—he'd run all the way around the globe if it meant she'd stay with him. And yet, she doubted him. He'd have to prove himself. Again. And again.

What was it Phego had said about trust? You can't convince someone to trust you; you can only act in a way that builds trust slowly. That proves who you are.

Obviously, Mammon was still in the proving phase.

But trust took time, and doubts cast long shadows. Ethan's betrayal had cut her deep. Far more than she would probably ever admit, but Mammon knew. He saw the emotional scars appear when she stopped fighting them, when she lost her focus and stared out at the horizon. When her beautiful face would drop the mask of indifference and become more expressive. The storm of those moments rolled through her the same way every time—pain at all she'd lost, at the lives taken from her by the selfishness of her last living relative. Next would come anger, fury even. Mammon assumed it was the memories of Ethan that caused that shift, but he never asked. She'd made it clear she wasn't ready to talk about that night, so he gave her space to work through things until she needed him. And she always needed him, because the last emotion, the final nail in the coffin, was the guilt that he knew ate at her. Those were the moments when he'd take her in his arms and hold her tight, growling low and soft in her ear to remind her he was there. He cared. He'd never let her go.

And sometimes he was enough to push the guilt aside. Not always, but more often than not. Mammon wasn't sure if she'd ever forgive herself for the explosion at the rescue and the two lost lives that night. He hoped, but there was no guarantee. Charmeine had been through too much to be easily swayed.

So instead of attacking her trust issues directly, Mammon went back to the foundation they'd built together. They'd started as enemies, but the lust between them had pushed them into bedfellows. The sex and desire had helped them grow as friends—and later as more. Lust was familiar and solid, never-ending, it seemed. Lust he could handle.

With nothing more than a growl in warning, Mammon grabbed the back of Charmeine's panties and yanked, ripping them from her hips. She jolted, her eyes going dark with her desire, the scent of her arousal growing thick and delicious. Yep, they had lust down pat.

"Are you my mate?" Mammon ran his fingers between them and over her pussy, loving the way she jumped and sighed when he hit all the right spots, how she groaned when he zeroed in on her clit.

"Yes." She grabbed his shirt, ripping it from the neckline down. Not that he cared. He loved it when she lost a little of that impressive control.

"Then why would you doubt I want to be with you?" Mammon licked the mark on her shoulder, the mating bite he'd given her only a few days ago. He wore a matching one on his neck. She'd wanted hers to be subtle, something she could disguise if need be. Something just for her. He'd wanted his bold and bright and right where the entire world could see it. Typical of the two of them, really.

Charmeine reached between them and unfastened his pants, pushing them off his hips. "I just…I hate that you have to give up your life for us to be together."

Mammon growled and bit her neck, not enough to break skin but enough to hold her. To make her freeze in his arms before he released her once more. "I'm giving up nothing. What I'm gaining in being able to be with you every day and to help the refugees more than makes up for any perceived slight at simply having to move."

"Your Dire Wolf brothers—"

He slid a finger inside her, loving the way her legs quivered. The way she gasped and dropped her head to his shoulder.

"My brothers live all over the country. This won't change anything."

Charmeine groaned and clutched at his shoulders, and his control broke. He loved her like this—all wild and free. Out of control. He loved knowing only he could push her to that point. He was a selfish bastard, but that didn't matter. She liked him that way. Got off on knowing how possessive he could be.

"Apparently, I've neglected this sweet pussy." Mammon pulled his hand from her and gripped himself instead, lining up. "I'm going to fuck you, and then I'm going to tell you again how much happier I am with you as my mate, then I might fuck you a second time. And if the message isn't clear, I'll keep fucking you until you're too exhausted to worry about such silly things."

Charmeine growled all low and sensual, running her claws down his arms. "You filthy beast."

But she didn't push him away—she never did. Instead, she wrapped her legs around his hips and pulled him closer.

Mammon knew her signs, understood her tells. She wanted this as much as he did, if not more. Thank the fates for that.

Giving in to his desires, he pressed inside her with a sigh. Sliding deep as she arched and spread her legs wider, opening herself up for him. And fuck, did she feel good as her pussy swallowed his cock. The two worked together, moving, writhing, clutching one another as they pushed each other toward completion. Mammon could barely keep up with her, a fact that only made the sex that much hotter. His mate wanted him, was pleased with him, and loved him. She didn't trust him implicitly yet, but they could work on that. He would make sure to show her, to prove to her, that he was a trustworthy male. And he'd keep working. He'd give her all the time she needed to learn to trust him because he was in this forever. Whatever he'd done to deserve her, he wanted to keep doing it. He wanted to earn every second with her.

They came together with whispered curses and groans, holding tight, Mammon closing his eyes as Charmeine's pussy clenched around him. Bliss. At least for a moment. Because if there was one thing he knew about Charmeine Byrne, it was that the woman's mind was never quiet for long.

"You know," Charmeine said even before she'd fully caught her breath. "Perhaps you were right."

Mammon chuckled and shook his head, trying to force the blood back up to his brain. "About what?"

His mate didn't seem to have the same problem. "The blue. It does seem a bit too soft in this light."

Mammon growled and nipped at her shoulder, loving the way her pussy reacted with a soft aftershock. "This is what you think about right now? While I'm still inside you?"

She grinned, that secret pirate's smile she only ever gave him. "No. Normally, I think about how soon until you can make me come again."

Mammon spun away from the wall and dropped to his knees, taking her with him. Laying her out on the wood floor and covering her with his body.

"How soon would you want another orgasm?"

Charmeine fisted his hair, tugging his head down. Making her point clear. "That's a silly question."

Fuck, Mammon loved it when she got demanding. He slipped down between her spread legs, letting her push him where she wanted him. Letting her lead him. And when he got into the right spot, when her swollen, rosy pussy lay directly in front of his face, he wrapped his lips around her clit and sucked.

She rocked her hips against his face, making desire stir within him. Never enough. He would never get enough of his mate looking at him like she was right then. Disheveled, windblown even, with pink cheeks and full lips from his kisses. Staring down at him as if he was the best thing that had ever happened to her. And maybe he was. She was definitely the best thing that had happened in his very long life.

"Greedy man," she whispered, her eyes dark and filled with lust. Mammon chuckled against her before sliding two fingers inside her. Teasing her.

"For you, Char. Only for you."

Also *Available*

FERAL BREED MOTORCYCLE CLUB
Claiming His Fate
Claiming His Need
Claiming His Witch
Claiming His Beauty
Claiming His Fire
Claiming His Desire

FERAL BREED FOLLOWINGS
Claiming His Chance
Claiming His Prize
Claiming His Grace

THE GATHERING
Killian & Lyra
Gideon & Kalie
Blasius, Dante, & Moira
Blasius, Dante, & Moira: Homecoming

About
the Author

A storyteller from the time she could talk, *USA Today* bestsellng author Ellis grew up among family legends of hauntings, psychics, and love spanning decades. Those stories didn't always have the happiest of endings, so they inspired her to write about real life, real love, and the difficulties therein. From farmers to werewolves, store clerks to witches—if there's love to be found, she'll write about it. Ellis lives in the Chicago area with her husband, daughters, and to tiny fish that take up way too much of her time.

www.ellisleigh.com